"Have you ever made love in an elevator?" Ken whispered in her ear

"I—" Lisa couldn't get the words out when Ken's hand snaked down her back, under the waistband of her skirt. He was crossing the line, and she stood up straighter, almost unwilling to believe Ken was seducing her in a semipublic place. "Ken, not here."

"Yes, here." His fingers teased her, dipping beneath the band of her bikini panties. "You said everything and everything, remember?" he reminded her in a husky tone as he cupped her backside more intimately, stroking her, tempting her. Lisa's knees went weak and she had to grab the handrail for support. "Did you lie?" he asked.

"N-no." Someone else's voice. Unfamiliar and raspy. But Lisa didn't care. Whatever Ken's game was, he was winning.

He thrust his hips forward and she writhed shamelessly against his hard body, silently begging for more. Lost in an erotic haze, she rested her head against the cool glass walls of the elevator.

Glass? Her eyes flew open. "Ken!" She tried to wriggle free. "This is a glass elevator!"

A slow grin spread across his face. "That's what makes it so much fun...."

Blaze™

Dear Reader,

I love big cities. The thrum of energy, the sensual beat...the infinite possibilities around every corner. I lived in Los Angeles for four years and loved every minute of it. Setting my first Blaze novel in that fabulous city was a huge thrill for me. Since it was a Blaze title, I needed to find characters with an extremely sensual story to tell. And since it was set in L.A., I wanted characters with jobs that represented the two things the city is known for—food and film.

Lisa and Ken's story is one of lost love and reconciliation... along with a fair bit of sensual revenge! These two are professionals whose passion for their career is almost as strong as the passion in their personal lives. So when Lisa returns to Ken needing a favor— five years after she walked out on him—the tension under the surface is undeniable...and the chemistry between them is inescapable. He agrees to help...for a price. And I assure you, it's a price that will leave you breathless!

I'd love to hear what you think of my contribution to the SEXY CITY NIGHTS miniseries. Write to me at P.O. Box 151417, Austin, TX 78715-1417. Or you can visit my Web site at www.juliekenner.com to see what else I've got in the works! And don't forget to check out www.tryblaze.com!

Enjoy,

Julie Kenner

Books by Julie Kenner

HARLEQUIN TEMPTATION
772—NOBODY DOES IT BETTER
801—RECKLESS
840—INTIMATE FANTASY

L.A. CONFIDENTIAL

Julie Kenner

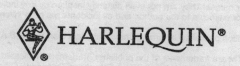

HARLEQUIN®

TORONTO • NEW YORK • LONDON
AMSTERDAM • PARIS • SYDNEY • HAMBURG
STOCKHOLM • ATHENS • TOKYO • MILAN • MADRID
PRAGUE • WARSAW • BUDAPEST • AUCKLAND

For Tim…who makes a mean plate of migas.

ISBN 0-373-79020-1

L.A. CONFIDENTIAL

Copyright © 2001 by Julia Beck Kenner.

Prologue

"MARK MY WORDS," Lisa Neal heard the bartender say. "Within five years, everyone in Los Angeles will be falling all over themselves to get a table at a Kenneth Harper restaurant."

Lisa had been sitting with her back leaning against the mahogany bar, her eyes scanning the crowd for Ken, but now she twisted her stool around. Behind the bar, Chris was shaking a martini and talking to a polished-looking redhead who seemed both fascinated and slightly intoxicated.

"Seriously," Chris said, "for someone from a hick town in Texas, the man's a marvel. He knows exactly where he wants to be, and he'll get there, too."

Lisa couldn't help but smile. After dating Ken for close to a year, she had no doubt that what Chris said was true. Still, she couldn't resist teasing the bartender, and she leaned closer. "Chris, I'm shocked. Five years? Awfully disloyal, don't you think? Three seems much more likely."

"He's not you, Lisa," he said dryly. "I figure you'll be getting your first Academy Award this week."

She laughed. Sadly, seven days was a little fast

even for the career schedule she'd worked out in her head. "Considering I just finished shooting my thesis film this morning, maybe we should make that a month."

"Slacker."

She made a face and tapped her wineglass, which he topped off before turning back to the redhead. Lisa genuinely liked Chris. For that matter, she liked all the people Ken had recruited to work in Oxygen, his very first restaurant. From what she could tell, he'd chosen his people well. Tonight's opening gala had been *the* event of the summer, and it was going over without a hitch. The place was hopping with minor celebrities and celebrity wanna-bes. Cameras were flashing, the crowd was buzzing, and the smell of celebration—not to mention exceptional food—filled the air.

Earlier, a restaurant critic from the *Los Angeles Times* had come to their table and personally congratulated Ken. Of course, Lisa hadn't expected anything less. After all, Ken's talent and drive was one of the things that had attracted her in the first place. Ken Harper's ambition equaled her own, and that was a rare trait indeed.

Not that she was interested in settling down, but if she were, it would be with a man like Ken. She took a long sip of wine, realizing with a start how completely happy she'd been over the past eleven months. *Amazing.*

Ken had snuck up on her, and for the first time in her life, she didn't mind feeling committed to a man.

Not that she intended to get all mushy. Not now, when her career was about to take off. In the real world, what mattered was success, and Lisa had been just as pragmatic in choosing a relationship as she had in choosing a graduate school.

Her whole life she'd accomplished whatever she set her mind to. Valedictorian of her high school class. Editor of the yearbook. The state essay contest. She knew from watching her own family how important goals were. Her mom had given up a legal career on Wall Street to live in Idaho with her dad, and then he'd up and left after Lisa and her sister, Ellen, started high school. A single mom with two kids, Lisa's mother wasn't exactly up to going back to New York, so she'd ended up trapped—and resenting the hell out of Lisa's father. And all because she'd sacrificed her career for a man.

Lisa's sister didn't have it much better. Ellen had married a nice enough guy, but she was trapped in that same small town just because her husband owned a local hardware store. So instead of traveling the world and shooting photos of exotic locales for fancy magazines as could have been her fate, Ellen worked part-time at a department store, shooting portraits of kids who really didn't want to be there.

Maybe Ellen was happy—she said she was—but Lisa didn't ever intend to do that to herself. She'd had her life mapped out from day one, and she intended to follow through. That's who she was, and she never intended to lose sight of that fact.

Still, Ken was as close to a soul mate as she'd ever

found—could ever imagine finding, for that matter. And every day they spent together drew them a little bit closer. For a loner like Lisa that was scary, but it was exciting, as well.

She shifted on the stool, scanning the crowd without success to find him. For a moment she wondered if he'd disappeared into the kitchen. Then a man in a dark blue suit moved aside, and suddenly there Ken was. She took a deep breath, her pulse quickening when he caught her eye and the corner of his mouth turned up in a secret smile meant only for her.

Two years older than Lisa, Ken had just turned twenty-six. Even so, he commanded the room. His clear blue eyes looked every guest in the face, his firm handshake making each feel welcome and comfortable. Lisa knew from experience that those hands were callused and rough, but that would only serve to endear him to the public. Though his classic good looks might suggest otherwise, Ken wasn't a man who shied away from hard work.

His tailored silk suit wasn't pretentious, but neither was it off the rack, and the ensemble gave him a cultured yet accessible quality that Lisa was sure would attract the clientele in droves. As Ken was fond of saying, in the restaurant industry, the food had to be perfect. And everything else—the space, the service, the ambience—had to live up to that standard.

His eyes never left hers as he moved easily through the crowd until he was by her side, his hand warm against her bare back as he dipped his head to kiss her cheek. "Have I told you how beautiful you look tonight?" His feather-soft whisper teased her senses.

Pressing her forefinger to her lip, she pretended to consider. "Mmm. Let's see…gorgeous, stunning, amazing. But no, not beautiful."

He moved behind her, his hands resting on her shoulders as he leaned close. "You're beautiful."

She grinned. "And you're a charmer."

"True," he said, sliding onto the stool next to her. "But I'm an honest charmer."

He signaled to Chris, who brought him a sparkling water with lime, and then Ken started asking the bartender's opinion of how the opening was going. She watched as the two men talked, impressed once again with the life that was hers since she'd moved to Los Angeles.

She'd shocked everyone in her small Idaho hometown when she'd applied for early admission to U.C.L.A. and moved to the big, bad city right after her junior year of high school. Of course, the move hadn't come as any huge surprise for her mother. After all, Lisa'd spent her entire life with her face behind a lens—first her grandfather's ancient Super8, and then the school's video camera. Still, her mom had been nervous about her firstborn moving to California at seventeen.

She'd done them proud, though. She finished her undergrad work in a little under three years and was immediately accepted into the graduate film program. Long hours, intense competition, relentless professors…and she'd loved every minute of it. In fact, her life would have been nothing *but* school if she hadn't met Ken.

They'd met at a party, and so far their lives meshed perfectly. Ken was as involved with his restaurant as she was with her films. Their rare free time they spent together, and Lisa had become accustomed to sitting at one of the empty tables at Oxygen studying or annotating a script while Ken worked out details with the construction crew or his staff.

They'd become comfortable together, and she liked the feeling. In so many ways the relationship was different than what she'd had with her past boyfriends. For one thing, he insisted that he didn't want to have sex until after marriage, although they'd done everything but.

Lisa found it hard to believe that a man as sexy and alluring as Ken was a virgin, but she'd never asked him outright if that was the case. Rather, she'd agreed with his parameters. She adored Ken, but she didn't intend to let anything—including thoughts of marriage—get between her and her goal of making it in the movie business. And if that meant keeping some tiny modicum of distance between them, well, so be it.

She took another sip of wine, watching as Ken finished chatting with Chris. Then he turned back to her and tucked a stray strand of hair behind her ear, the simple gesture somehow more intimate that a kiss.

"Beautiful," he whispered, as she fought a blush. She usually pulled her annoyingly thick hair back in a ponytail, but for tonight, she'd gone all out and had it done up in a chignon by the hotel's stylist. She had to admit, it looked great. "How are you holding up?" he asked. "Tired?"

"Not at all."

He raised an eyebrow in disbelief. "You haven't slept in days. Are you sure you're not a tiny bit tired?"

While Ken had been readying for his opening, she'd been awake for two solid days shooting the last few scenes of her thesis film. She'd pushed her actors and crew hard, but they'd delivered.

Maybe it was simply a student film, but she was producing and directing it, and that was more than just a baby step. It was a giant leap toward the one thing she'd wanted for her whole life—producing real, honest-to-goodness Hollywood movies. "I'm operating on adrenaline. My film, your restaurant. I've got energy to burn."

"Glad to hear it." He looked away for a moment to wave at someone across the room, and when he looked back, his stormy-blue eyes were dark with undisguised passion. "I was hoping you'd have some energy left over after this is through." He pressed a card key into her hand. "The hotel put me in the penthouse for the night. If you get tired, head on up and I'll meet you there."

She nodded, clutching the key in her hand as he bent and kissed her. He tasted of champagne, and she trembled as she pulled his head closer to her own, deepening their kiss even as she fought the sudden prick of tears at her eyes. Ken worked some mysterious alchemy on her soul, and she knew that if she let him get too close, he was the one person in the world for whom she'd consider abandoning her dreams.

In a way, the knowledge was warm and reassuring. But, mostly, it terrified her.

He pulled away, one finger under her chin tilting her head up. "You okay?"

"Fine." She smiled. "I'm terrific."

"I need to go mingle." He presented his arm. "Care to join me?"

"You go on. I guess I am a little tired. I just want to sit here and watch everyone fawn over you."

The corner of his mouth twitched. "I'll see you in a bit, then."

As soon as he moved away, the crowd engulfed him. Yes, Chris was right. In five years, Ken Harper was going to be the uncontested king of the Los Angeles restaurant scene.

She turned back to the bar, then took an idle sip of wine.

"Something wrong?"

She looked into Chris's concerned face, then realized she was frowning. "No. I'm fine. Just tired."

He looked dubious, but one of the waitresses came to the service area, and he left to fill her orders. In truth, she wasn't fine. Ken was firmly on his path to success, but she was on the verge of graduating and still hadn't found decent work. She'd had offers, of course, but mostly the jobs had involved working long hours as part of the crew for a low-budget film.

Not bad for starting out, but Lisa wanted to be a development executive at one of the major studios before she was thirty—and with a goal like that, she needed to land a stellar, high-profile job right out of the gate.

Unfortunately, she hadn't yet found one.

Determined to pull herself out of her funk, she twisted back around to watch the crowd. She tried to find Ken, but instead found herself sucking in a startled breath when she saw Drake Tyrell—one of the country's hottest independent producers—heading right toward her.

"Miss Neal." He slipped onto the empty stool next to her, then signaled to Chris to freshen his drink. Through the whole process, she just sat there gaping, awed that he even remembered who she was. "It's good to see you again."

She swallowed. "Thank you. Sir. I mean...it's good to see you, too." She fought a cringe, knowing she sounded like a tongue-tied fool. "I'm surprised you remember me." He'd taught a weekend seminar, and she'd been one of two hundred students crammed into a small auditorium. Hardly the opportunity to stand out.

"Of course I remember." Chris brought him a fresh drink and he raised the glass to toast. "To successfully getting through film school. Hell of an accomplishment."

They clinked glasses, and he leaned back, eyeing her speculatively. Her nerves were about to shift into overdrive when he said, "I read your script."

"Only Angels?"

When he nodded, her stomach twisted. She wondered not only why he'd read the thing, but what he'd thought of it. She'd written it more than a year ago and entered it in a contest at her professor's urging.

"I'm one of the sponsors of the fellowship program," he said, answering one of her unasked questions. "You have a flair for comedy. The script was charming."

Her smile felt as watery as her knees, and she kept a firm hold on the back of the bar stool. "I'm glad you thought so," she said, thrilled to find her voice was functioning. "It didn't win," she added, then immediately kicked herself for sounding petty.

He laughed, and she felt even smaller, at least until he said, "Not the fellowship, no." He leaned closer, in front of her to grab a napkin off the bar. "But it just may have won you a job."

At that, she almost lost her balance, and she grabbed onto the solid mahogany of the bar. "Excuse me?"

"I've been talking with your professors, looking over your work. I've got a job for you, if you want it."

"A job?" she repeated stupidly. "Working with you?"

His grin was slow—probably he was used to people being in utter awe of him. "Of course. That is, if you think you're up for it."

Up for it? Of course she was up for it. The one thing she wanted most in the world had just been dropped in her lap. *A job.* A real career working with *the* Drake Tyrell.

"Of course, you'll have to move to New York."

She blinked. "Of course," she murmured, trying not to scowl. How stupid of her to not have realized right off. As did Woody Allen and a handful of other producer/directors, Tyrell worked out of New York, refusing to set foot in Los Angeles unless absolutely necessary.

She didn't have a clue why he avoided California. Fear of earthquakes, an allergy to smog, an intense hatred of freeways…who knew? Didn't much matter. The bottom line for her was simple—work for Tyrell, move to New York. Cut, mark it, that's a wrap.

He watched her, silent, not pressing, but neither did he offer to give her time to make up her mind. People like Tyrell expected action—folks jumped when they said "Boo." If she wanted the job, she had to let him know before he walked away. Every instinct in her body told her to jump at the chance. This was her career, after all.

And then there was Ken.

Her eyes welled, and she blinked back the tears, annoyed with herself for being so emotional. She made a point of being perfectly sensible where her career was concerned, but that didn't change the fact that she and Ken had become remarkably close, and it was going to tear her up inside to move so far away.

But she'd worked her tail off for years—all with the goal of one day being a full-fledged player in the Hollywood scene. She had to grab her chance while she could. Opportunity was pounding on her door; she needed to open the dead bolt and let it in.

Surely Ken would understand. After all, just this very night he'd taken the first step toward realizing his own ambition. And it wasn't as if they were engaged or anything. Besides, she wasn't breaking up with him, just moving away. She'd come back when she'd made something of a name for herself—hopefully sooner rather than later.

The bottom line was, she had to take the job. If she didn't, for the rest of her life she'd wonder "What if?"

"Lisa?" At Tyrell's voice, she sat up straighter, pulling her thoughts together into one cohesive package. "Are you interested?"

A real job, working for Drake Tyrell. Scary, but undeniably enticing. *And everything you've ever dreamed of wrapped up in one package.* There was no way she could say no, no way at all. This was her dream. *Her life.*

Taking a deep breath to calm the butterflies in her stomach, she looked Drake in the eyes. "Absolutely." She held out her hand for him to shake. "I won't disappoint you."

1

Five years later...

AS ALWAYS during the lunch rush, every seat at Oxygen was full, and the hostess was issuing pagers to the intrepid souls who hadn't thought to make reservations and were now faced with a two-hour wait. At least at lunch they had the option of waiting. During the dinner hours those without reservations were politely turned away, and even clients with reservations usually waited at least half an hour.

The difficulty in getting a table didn't seem to bother the patrons. For that matter, it seemed to add to the clamor to be among those who dined regularly at the trendy restaurant—which, of course, was exactly what Ken had planned.

Still, the crowds were intense, and when he had first realized just how huge a success the restaurant was going to be, Ken had considered expanding. Brant Tucker, who owned the Bellisimo Hotel, had agreed to let the restaurant take over almost the entire mezzanine, and Ken had even gone so far as to hire an architect.

In the end, though, he'd decided to keep his firstborn just the way it was. More than one review had raved about the cozy atmosphere, and Ken wasn't inclined to take risks with the establishment that had literally launched his career.

Instead he'd compromised by opening a north location in Malibu and a south location in Marina Del Rey. With more capacity, the satellites were soon doing more business than the original location. But the first restaurant held a special place in Ken's heart. And even after he'd opened a half dozen other restaurants with different names, he spent most lunch hours and weekend nights at the original Oxygen.

There were days when he still couldn't get his mind around the extent of his success. Five years ago he'd mortgaged himself to the hilt to get it up and running, but he'd actually pulled it off—and in a big way. Not bad for a college dropout from Blanco, Texas. He wished his parents were still alive to see it, but he knew they'd have been proud.

It was his mother to whom he owed his success. She convinced his father to open a BBQ restaurant on the town square when Ken was just a toddler. He grew up in that kitchen, helping his mom when he could, getting underfoot and generally being a pest most of the time. But he saw how the town folk gravitated to the humble spot. And by the time he was in high school, On the Square had become the local after-school, after-work, after-church hangout.

It didn't take Ken long to realize he wanted to create something like that. A miniature town meeting hall. A place folks could come and enjoy the food, drink a little, dance a little, and have a good time.

He'd started out by studying business at the University of Texas, earning his tuition by working in every restaurant that would have him. At first he'd planned to open a simple restaurant in Austin, figuring its laid-back community would be perfect for what he'd had in mind.

But then one drunk driver had changed everything. Suddenly his parents were dead. His home had been ripped out from under him, and he'd felt more lost than he'd ever imagined possible. Uncomfortable in his own skin, he'd dropped out of college and escaped to the West coast, drowning his grief in a newly fueled ambition. He may have started out only wanting to operate a dive reminiscent of his mother's place, but he'd accomplished so much more. He'd become a rich man, powerful in the industry.

As usual, this afternoon he was moving among the tables, shaking hands and greeting the attorneys and brokers who made up the majority of the regular lunch crowd. He was chatting with a newly elected judge when he noticed one of the restaurant's publicists, Marty Talbot, waving at him from a two-top across the room. After excusing himself, Ken headed over, greeting a few regulars along the way.

"I didn't expect to see you today, Marty. I figured you'd be tired of me after we spent all day yesterday together in a conference room."

The older man chuckled, his silver-gray hair giving him a congenial appearance that belied his slick negotiating skills. "I never get tired of a man who pays my bills so promptly." Marty gestured to the empty

L.A. Confidential

seat, and Ken sat down. "Actually, Alicia asked me to pitch her show to you one more time."

Ken stifled a groan. A former news anchor, Alicia Duncan now had her own morning talk show. Apparently she didn't have anything better to fill the air with, so she'd taken to bugging Ken.

He shook his head, annoyed that he had to revisit what he'd thought was a dead issue. "I told both of you yesterday, I'm not interested."

"Fair enough. I just wanted to make sure you'd fully considered her proposition before turning it down."

"I've considered," Ken said, trying to hide his irritation.

"Have you?" Marty asked.

"Come on, Marty. You of all people should know how I feel about publicity." An old college friend of his father's, Marty had known Ken his entire life.

Marty waved his fork in Ken's direction. "Promotion's a good thing, son. It's not like you'd be falling in with the enemy."

"That's not the point. I built this restaurant up my way, and I've always advertised it my way. So far, I think my plan has worked like a charm."

All of his advertising focused on the food and the mystique that had grown up around the Oxygen name. No testimonials, no personal appearances, no tacky commercials filmed inside the restaurant, nothing that might diminish the aura that Ken had worked so hard to build.

And since every restaurant he'd launched had been

a remarkable success, Ken had no intention of now screwing with his advertising plan. As his dad used to say, "If it ain't broke, don't fix it."

Marty just shook his head and took another bite of salad without saying a word. Marty's habit of suddenly dropping out of conversations drove Ken crazy. And this time Ken was certain the older man was doing it on purpose, presumably to give Ken time to once again ponder Alicia's proposal.

One pernicious side effect of Ken's success was his semi-celebrity status—a status that unfortunately attracted the Alicias of the world. But just because the press now treated him as a celebrity, that didn't mean he had to encourage such nonsense. So when Alicia had suggested filming a segment of her show in the kitchen—and having the restaurant's hailed executive chef, Tim Sutton, whip up one of his famous creations on camera—Ken had flatly and resolutely said no. It wasn't an answer he intended to change, no matter how much Marty or Alicia pleaded.

Across from him, Marty finished his salad without saying a word. Not until the waiter slipped over and silently removed the empty plate, did Marty look up and meet Ken's eyes.

"Go ahead," Ken said, his voice resigned. Years of experience told him that there was no getting rid of Marty without first hearing him out. "Finish what you came here to say."

"It would bring in a broader clientele."

"I'm content with the clientele I've got."

"Then do it as a favor. For Alicia."

Ken ran his fingers through his hair, trying to figure out what the hell Marty was talking about. "Excuse me?"

Marty just shook his head, then ripped open a sugar packet and dumped it into his coffee.

The *clack* of the spoon against the coffee cup grated on Ken's nerves. "Marty…"

"Well, son, it's just that I think you ought to think of the girl," he said, signaling for a waiter, "especially after the way you two broke up."

Ken swallowed a burst of anger as he wondered what kind of nonsense Alicia had been spouting. "For one thing, we weren't dating. We went out to dinner twice. That doesn't make a relationship." They'd slept together, true, but both of them had known it wasn't going anywhere. "And even if we were, I'm not changing my philosophy for anybody. Not you, and certainly not Alicia. Nobody. I'm off limits. My restaurant's off limits. And that's just the way it is."

"If you're sure…"

A waiter, Jake, came over.

"I'm sure," Ken said.

"It would make a great tie-in with the anniversary. Five years next Saturday since you opened this place." He let the thought linger, then turned to Jake and started discussing the day's dessert selection.

Ken's stomach twisted. He knew perfectly well what day next Saturday was. Every year at this time he struggled through his own private hell. When the anniversary of Oxygen's opening rolled around, it was as if someone opened a memory floodgate and he was sucked out with the tide.

Five years ago he'd thought he had it so good. The opening of his first restaurant, a woman he adored and whom he thought adored him. But he'd been a fool. He'd stood right in this very room with an engagement ring in his pocket, so sure she wanted a life together as much as he did. Two days later, she'd left for New York with another man. Years later, the memory still rankled.

He'd wanted to wait until after they were married to make love, but apparently that wasn't enough for Lisa, and soon enough Ken heard the rumors and saw the pictures in the tabloids. She and Drake Tyrell were an item, a regular fixture in all the Manhattan hot spots.

The turn of events had completely sideswiped him—and Ken didn't consider himself anyone's fool.

What bothered him most, though, was that after five years, he still couldn't get her out of his head. If he saw her again, he didn't know if he'd want to run to her or away from her. He hoped the latter. The thought that, after so much time, Lisa Neal still had power over him was more than a little disturbing. And yet it was true. The woman had gotten under his skin and stayed there.

"I've decided to skip dessert," Marty said. "How about you? Have you made a decision about Alicia's program?"

Keeping his expression mild, Ken stood. "I'm skipping it, too," he said. "And this discussion is over." He told Jake to comp Marty's meal, then headed back through the tables toward the kitchen, needing some down time to relax and regroup.

Ken wasn't the type to feel sorry for himself, but one week out of the year didn't seem too outrageous an indulgence. The other fifty-one weeks he focused on his business and generally got on with his life. But despite the parade of women that came with his pseudo-celebrity status, so far he hadn't met a woman who affected him the way Lisa had. Half of him prayed that one day he would, so that he could finally forget about her. The other half wanted to hang on to the memory of her forever. Unfortunately, though, right on the heels of the memory was always the now-familiar anger that burned a hole in his gut every time he thought about the way she'd left him.

"I know that look," Tim said. "That's your one-week-before-the-anniversary look."

The familiar smells and sounds of the kitchen accosted his senses and lifted his spirits—the clatter of pots and pans, the sizzle of oil in a skillet, the gentle hiss of steam rising, the pungent aroma of minced garlic and diced onions. Despite himself, Ken's lips curved into a grin. "I think I'm entitled."

"Entitled? To what? To mope?" Tim looked up from where he was supervising his sous-chef, his face ruddy from the heat of the stove. Behind him, the assistants were doing prep work and the expeditor was finishing up the final orders for the latecomers to lunch.

"The woman I loved turned down a marriage proposal and told me she was moving to New York five years ago,'' Ken said, making sure his voice was low enough for only Tim. "A year later, she dumped me and shacked up with some Hollywood big shot. I think I'm entitled to a touch of melancholy."

Before Lisa left, Ken had been absolutely certain of the way his life was going to go down. He was going to live in a bungalow near the beach with his filmmaker wife and their beautiful kids, and they'd spend Sunday mornings trying to outdo each other with exotic and bizarre omelet variations. Weekend afternoons, they'd go see movies, then sit on the deck overlooking the ocean and analyze the heck out of the film they'd just seen while the kids played in the surf. During the evenings, he and Lisa would mingle among the Hollywood elite as they dined at a Ken Harper restaurant.

It had never once occurred to him that Lisa had a different view of the world.

Of course, they'd never seriously talked about marriage, although his insistence that they not sleep together until after they were married had meant that the topic had come up once or twice. The fact was, he'd wanted to bury himself inside of her more times than he could count. But he'd been down that road before, though never with a woman like Lisa. He'd thought she was special. He'd thought she was *the one*. And cliché or not, he'd wanted his ring on her hand before they'd shared a bed.

When she'd walked out, he'd been shaken to the very core. He'd begun to second-guess every decision as he lost the control he so prided himself on. His business acumen faltered, and he'd made some bad decisions. Decisions that had set him back months. He didn't intend to lose control like that ever again.

Tim was still staring at him, an almost sorrowful expression on his usually jovial face.

"What?" Ken demanded.

"You need to move on."

Ken crossed his arms and leaned against the stainless-steel prep area, trying to find a retort. But nothing came. Tim was right, but he didn't have the faintest idea how to go about it.

Lord knew, he'd cursed Lisa enough, especially on those rare occasions when he'd let the bitterness and humiliation get the better of him. He'd cursed and yelled and ranted until sheer exhaustion pulled him back. And still she was there, just under his skin. Part of him.

So how the hell could he move on?

Tim turned to Kelly, his sous-chef, then added some herbs from a nearby bowl to her roux, and Ken inhaled the wonderful scent. "Smells great," he said, partly to change to subject, but mostly because it was true.

"Of course." Tim's grin broadened shamelessly. "It's my recipe."

Ken let his gaze wander over the kitchen, not really seeing, as his thoughts drifted back to Lisa. "The thing is…" Ken trailed off, wishing he hadn't even opened his mouth.

"What?"

"Nothing."

Tim headed toward the stockroom, looking behind him to make sure Ken was following. "Spill it," he said when they were out of earshot of the rest of the staff.

"It's just…I don't know. I guess, when I think about her, even after all this time, I'm furious with her…but I also wonder what the hell I did wrong. You know. What I should have done differently."

"I repeat—you need to move on."

Ken brushed aside the comment. "I know, I know. But I'm not just talking about her. I'm talking about me. Not just with Lisa, but with my life." The truth was, she'd left him with a legacy of self-doubt, and it burned.

"Never second-guess yourself because of a woman, my friend. That's the path to an early grave—or at least a psychotic episode."

Ken chuckled. "Yeah? Well, you may be right about that."

"And speaking of moving on…I interviewed the cutest pastry chef last week." Tim kept his expression totally serious as he checked a produce list. "Now there's a cream puff—"

"Knock it off," Ken said with a grin.

Tim cracked a smile. "Just watching out for my best friend. You should date more."

"Me? You're the one who hasn't had a date since Melinda left. I've had so many dates I should buy stock in a little black book company."

"First," Tim said as they left the stockroom and

headed for the break room, "we're not talking about me. Second, you haven't had dates, you've had physical encounters. Hit-and-run dating."

He poured himself a cup of coffee and sat at the Formica-topped table, his large, former-NFL-linebacker body looking out of place on the small chair. If his knee hadn't blown out, Tim probably would have made it far in football...and Ken would be out one hell of a chef.

"I mean, have you tried to get to know any of those women?" Tim asked.

Ken cocked his head and tried to look stern. "I can't say I'm comfortable being psychoanalyzed while my head chef sits in the break room right as the lunch rush is wrapping up."

"No?" Tim took another slug of coffee. "Well, I'm a perfectionist, you know. And I don't think I can work until I'm sure you aren't making a mess out of your life."

Ken pinched the bridge of his nose, half in irritation and half in amusement. "I appreciate your concern, but my life is fine. I'm not holed up in some dark room pining away for Lisa. I hardly think about her—"

Tim snorted.

"—except for this time of year. And I *am* dating."

"You're not seeing anyone seriously."

"Neither are you."

"We're not—"

"Talking about you. I know. But maybe we should."

"It's only been a year," Tim said. "And it's not like I have a ton of free time."

"Touché."

Tim sighed and drummed his fingers on the table. "All right. You win. But just tell me one thing." He looked Ken in the eye and waited for his nod. "You doin' okay?"

"Sure," Ken said, not sure if it was the truth or a lie. "I'm absolutely fine."

ALICIA DUNCAN hated to fail. Particularly when the failure was known, as was this most recent setback. Now she sat perfectly straight in front of the mirror as her producer poured out his litany of complaints. A ponytailed bimbette fussed near her, supposedly fixing Alicia's makeup, but clearly eavesdropping.

Well, wasn't that just great? The bimbette would probably run to the phone the second Alicia left, and soon enough the gossip would be everywhere—Alicia was on the outs with her producer because she couldn't land a piddly-ass little story about restaurant mogul Ken Harper. What made the defeat even more grating was that she and Ken had actually dated last summer, but he still wouldn't do her this one favor.

She closed her eyes and pressed a finger to her temple. She'd won two Emmys, for crying out loud. She really didn't need this garbage.

"Have you even heard a word I've said?" Gavin's irritated voice filtered through her thoughts, and she looked up, the reflection of her eyes meeting his in the lighted mirror.

"I don't need to hear your every word, sweetie. I got your point twenty minutes ago when you first opened your mouth." The bimbette dabbed her forehead with a powder puff, and Alicia jerked forward, glaring. "You. Out. Now."

The girl backed away, her eyes wide, her teeth digging into her lower lip.

"And if you say a word about this to anyone, it'll be your job." She flashed her most charming smile, the one that had gotten her an anchor slot on a network affiliate. "Understand?"

The girl nodded, then escaped out the door. Alicia took a deep breath, then spun her chair around to face Gavin.

The corner of his mouth twitched. "You certainly have a way with people."

"Don't give me any crap. I'm in a bad mood, and you're on my list." She had better things to do than to sit and listen to Gavin complain about how she hadn't managed to land a story. Especially since this story, about the fifth anniversary of Oxygen, was such an uninteresting fluff piece. Ken had flat-out refused her offer to have him and his chef on the program. A little banter, a little cooking demonstration. Lightweight stuff, and great publicity for him.

"So why'd he say no?"

"How the hell should I know?" His refusal had totally pissed her off, but she wasn't about to admit that to Gavin. Instead, she just squinted toward the mirror then ran her finger under her lip, wiping off a stray bit of lipstick. "He's an idiot?"

"I don't think so. The man clawed his way up from nothing to become the hottest restaurateur in Southern California. I suspect at least a modicum of savvy, if not downright intelligence."

She bit back a snarl, not interested in analyzing Ken Harper. "Who cares? He doesn't want to do it. End of story."

"Is it?"

She twisted around to look him in the eye. "Why are you so intent on going after Ken Harper?"

Gavin shook his head. "I'm not. I'm intent on going after a story. Harper's been the unchallenged king of cuisine for years, yet no one's ever managed to get him to consent to an interview inside his restaurant. We manage that, we get ratings. We get ratings, you get a better slot." He held his hands out to his side. "I'm only thinking of you, babe."

"It's only worth pursuing if there's a story, Gavin. The man's as dull as dishwater." A lie, especially if they were talking about in bed. But she wasn't feeling particularly charitable at the moment.

"Or maybe you didn't want to return to the place of your former defeat."

That was another reason Gavin drove her nuts—he knew her just a little too well. "Don't be ridiculous. We went out a couple of times, but I dumped him," she lied. "Believe me, Ken Harper isn't even in my league."

"So what's stopping you from doing the story?"

"There is no story."

"Are you sure?"

Irritated, she spun the chair back to face the mirror and saw him watching her in the reflection. She hated admitting it, but maybe Gavin was right. Maybe Ken was hiding something. If he was, it would feel damn good to be the reporter who aired the remarkable Ken Harper's dirty laundry.

"Or maybe you *do* think it's out of your league?"

"Not hardly," she said tightly as she made up her mind. She met his eyes in the mirror and smiled sweetly. "You want the dirt on Harper? Then that's exactly what you'll get."

2

THE MANHATTAN OFFICE of Avenue F Films was more spartan than Lisa had expected. A polished metal-and-glass table served as a reception desk, and a few uncomfortable-looking chairs made up the waiting area. An Oriental-style tapestry covered one wall, while the other was decorated with geometrically shaped mirrors. At the far end of the room, frosted-glass panels separated the reception area from the boss's lair. Overall, the room gave the impression of too much money and not enough taste.

Lisa grimaced. She wasn't there to criticize Winston Miller's decorating skills; she was there to interview for a much needed job. The place could be knee-deep in seventies-style shag, and she wouldn't complain.

Her back straight, she moved forward, letting the frosted-glass door—complete with an ornately etched F—swing quietly shut. She flashed what she hoped was a confident smile at the receptionist, then waited for the girl to finish her phone call. When the petite redhead finally looked up, Lisa's pasted-on smile had almost faded. ''I'm Lisa Neal, Mr. Miller's four o'clock.''

Apparently not one for conversation, the receptionist gestured toward one of the torture-chamber chairs,
her attention now directed at her fingernails. Lisa
checked her watch. Four o'clock on the dot. "Is
he—"

"Running late," the girl said, pulling a nail file
from a drawer. "Just have a seat."

Great. Lisa moved across the room toward the
chairs, glancing at her reflection in the mirrors as she
walked. The chin-length bob she wore had the benefit
of not only being easy to fix, but of looking professional. The suit was a cheap designer knockoff, and
the shoes were leftovers of her more cash-flush days.
Still, the outfit was sharp enough that it bolstered the
businesswoman look. Overall, not too bad, all things
considered.

As much as she hated needing work, she hated even
more *looking* like she needed work. So much so that
she'd almost splurged and put a new outfit on her one
credit card that still had some room. But common
sense had won out. She hadn't worked steadily in
more than a year, and the money she made from
temping didn't justify a new outfit, especially when
she might need her credit card to buy food.

Still, the whole dress-for-success concept made a
lot of sense, and yesterday after she'd received her
best friend Greg's message that he'd landed her an
interview with Winston Miller, Lisa'd spent an entire
afternoon prowling the garment district for something
that would at least make it look as if she wasn't des-
titute. One thing she'd learned after years of working

on the fringes of the entertainment industry, the more someone looked as though they needed the work, the less likely they were to get it.

Smoothing her skirt, she sat on the hideous chair, her tailbone boring into the hard metal. She pulled her Day-Timer planner out of her purse and tried to look as if she had a schedule to keep. She wished she knew more about what Winston needed, but Greg had only left a note on the refrigerator. Though they shared an apartment, they were hardly ever home at the same time, and since he was in the middle of rehearsing for an off-off-off-off Broadway show, she'd been unable to catch him before the interview.

She shot a glance toward the receptionist, who didn't even look her way. So Lisa spent the next thirty minutes doodling and making anagrams out of her name, until she'd wasted so much time she was beginning to get irritated. Trying for haughty, she stood up, tucked her planner under her arm, and marched toward the anorexic receptionist.

The woman blinked, but didn't say a word.

"It's been almost an hour," Lisa said, trying to remain polite. "I have other meetings that I really can't—"

"No problem."

"Great. Thanks."

The girl poised her pen over the open appointment book. "When would you like to reschedule?"

"Oh, uh," Lisa stammered. "I guess I'll have to check my schedule."

The girl raised an eyebrow and waited, and Lisa

knew perfectly well that Miller's receptionist wasn't buying it. The question now was, did she keep her pride and walk out, or did she fall to her knees and beg?

"Well?" the girl asked, the end of her pen tapping the appointment book.

"Right." Lisa started flipping pages. She'd reschedule for tomorrow. That way she'd lose twenty-four hours in her job hunt, but she'd save a tiny bit of pride. "How about tomorrow?"

"No go." The girl trailed the tip of the pen down the page, then flipped over a few days. "I can squeeze you in next Tuesday."

So much for pride. Time for some serious begging. "Um, listen—"

"Miss Neal!"

She spun toward the source of the nasal voice, thrilled to be getting a reprieve from her fib.

"Come in, come in." Winston Miller practically bounded toward her, shook her hand heartily, then led her back into his office. "Sorry to keep you waiting. Been on the phone with Los Angeles all morning."

Lisa stifled a smile. As far as she knew, there were several million people in L.A.; she doubted Miller had been chatting with all of them.

"So, Greg tells me you're the man for this job." He motioned her toward a cushy chair as he slid behind his desk. "I understand you've got quite a range of experience."

"That's true," she said, wondering how much her friend had told him. She'd known Greg for almost

five years, ever since he'd had a bit part in a Drake
Tyrell film that she'd associate produced. Flamboyant
and opinionated, Greg had a wicked sense of humor
that got her through some rough times during filming,
and they'd spent hours eating bad food at the craft
services table. By the time the shoot was over, they'd
become fast friends and roommates.

Only Greg knew how scattershot her production
experience had been. Certainly, she'd never told her
family how bad times had become. From script su-
pervisor to art director to property master, she'd held
all sorts of jobs she'd never expected and didn't want.
Hardly what she'd anticipated five years ago when
she'd followed Tyrell to New York with delusions of
producing award-winning films. Still, the odd jobs
paid the bills—at least until recently when work had
seemed to dry up. Now, though, she couldn't imagine
which aspect of her background Greg thought was
worthy of Miller's attention.

Miller leaned back, his leather chair squeaking.
"What did Greg tell you about the job?"

"He told me you're producing a sequel to *The Velvet Bed* and that you've got some key positions to
fill." The erotic adventure, set in Manhattan's hot
spots, had been a surprise hit, solidifying Avenue F's
reputation as the most important independent film
company in the business.

"Half right. I am doing the sequel." He picked a
stack of paper up off his desk and riffled the pages.
"I want to start production in about nine months."

"Oh." Lisa tried to hide her confusion. "Greg

thought you might have a position for me. If you're still putting together your team, I've got several associate producer credits—"

"From when you were with Tyrell?"

"Well, yeah."

He nodded but didn't say anything, and she felt a familiar surge of anger rise to the surface. Never in a million years would she have guessed that simply being associated with Tyrell would have so sullied her reputation. But it was her own damn fault. She'd been a naive little girl from Idaho when she'd left Los Angeles with stars in her eyes, so sure that working for Tyrell would put her on the path to fame and fortune.

She'd thought he admired her talent, and by the time she was settled in Manhattan, she'd thought he genuinely cared for her. But Tyrell didn't care for anyone but himself, and back then she'd just been too starry-eyed to see it. Now she had to live with the backlash from her foolishness, and it drove her nuts that her career was tainted because Tyrell had thrown his life down the toilet.

The whole thing had been a huge scandal. One of the major Hollywood studios had pumped a ton of money into one of Tyrell's films—a picture everyone involved expected to be a blockbuster. About the time they were supposed to start production, Tyrell started snorting the budget up his nose—and then demanding more money from the studio. He shot some footage, but it was garbage, and eventually the studio shut the project down. Tyrell's company filed bankruptcy, and Tyrell fled to London in disgrace.

In the film world it was a debacle of *Heaven's Gate* proportions. And, unfortunately, Lisa had a producer credit. No real power, of course, since Tyrell never let go of control, but by the time she'd learned about Tyrell's drug problem and realized he was sinking fast, she'd been stuck. And now her reputation was just as smeared as his.

Miller was still looking at her with that expression of distrust she knew well from so many job interviews. Tyrell had screwed her, and good.

She tried to tamp down her anger. "I've worked my tail off, and I'm good. After I left Tyrell, I produced and directed at Cornerstone." Of course, her films had a shoestring budget, lots of car explosions, and went straight to video, but it was something. Goodness knows, that was what she'd told her mom every time she'd called. "After Cornerstone went under, I got a crew position on one of the late-night network talk shows. And for the last year, I've been working a variety of jobs in the industry."

She didn't mention that she'd been laid off from the network job due to budget cuts, that lately "variety" meant temping at video rental stores, and that she was now trying her damnedest to get some work lined up in Los Angeles so that she could move back to the coast and start over with her film career. "I'm perfectly qualified. No matter what—"

"Location scout."

She blinked, trying to follow the conversation. Was he suggesting she work as his scout? Track down the various locations for his next film and get commitments from the property owners? Except for her thesis film and a music video a friend had produced and directed years ago, she'd never done any scouting. "I'm not sure I'm—"

"If I like your work, I'll set you up as my line producer."

She snapped her mouth shut, overlooking her irritation at the way he kept interrupting her. The line producer was in charge of the day-to-day operations once filming got under way. Not a bad job, but not her ambition. She wanted to be doing the big-picture stuff. Working with writers and directors. Pulling the project together and getting the financing off the ground. The nitty-grit stuff. The fun stuff.

Still, if he was willing to bargain, maybe she could wrangle a job that would put her back on the map. "I'm not interested in line producer," she said slowly, knowing her gamble was risky.

He peered at her, the flesh on his forehead creasing. "I'm not sure we're communicating here. You won't be my *anything* unless you're my scout. And even then, only if you do the quality job I need."

She shook her head, unable to figure out why he'd be so gung-ho on having her scout his locations. "Why me?"

Miller shrugged. "Greg assured me you're the one I need. He's a good actor, a good friend, and I trust the kid."

"But...I...." She sat up straighter, trying to regroup. What on earth was Greg thinking?

"He tells me you lived in L.A. Know it like the back of your hand."

"Los Angeles?" He wasn't making sense. "I haven't lived in Los Angeles in years." Sad, but true. And Greg knew it. She was missing something, but she didn't know what.

The look of anticipation on his face faded, only to be replaced with a cold, wary expression, as if now he couldn't quite figure out what she was doing there. Too late, Lisa realized her mistake. *The Velvet Bed* had been set in Manhattan's hot spots, combining the fictional erotic journey of the lead characters with the real Manhattan landscape. The combination of the real and the fictitious had sparked nationwide interest and certainly contributed to the film's unexpected success. Miller hadn't said so out loud, but Lisa would bet money that the sequel would follow the same formula—only this time in L.A.

Which meant she'd just blown her chance at getting the job Greg had so carefully lined up for her. *Damn.*

"I'm going to set the sequel in either San Francisco or Los Angeles, depending on where I can lock in the more interesting locations. Of course, my preference is Los Angeles, and Greg seemed to think you could help with L.A. But if you don't know the city—"

"Oh, I know it. I lived there for years."

He looked dubious. "I need someone who knows it today."

"I know Los Angeles," she repeated. "I go back all the time." That was a flat-out lie, and she hoped he didn't call her on it. She appeased her guilt simply because she knew that if she got the job she wouldn't rest until she really did know everything there was to know about the City of Angels.

He nodded, but didn't say a word. Then he slipped a cigar out of a humidor on his desk, cut off the end, and lit up without asking if she minded. She did, but she kept her mouth shut. After a few puffs he aimed the cigar at her. "I'm gonna be straight with you."

"I appreciate that," she said, trying to keep her tone even.

"I keep my office in New York, but I know people on the coast." He leaned over, gesturing with the cigar. "Finding a location scout's not a problem. Finding a scout who can get me access to the places I want to be...that's another story."

She tried to play it cool as her mind raced ahead at a thousand miles an hour, trying to figure out what the devil Greg could have told him. What places in Los Angeles did he think she had special access to? "What locations are you interested in?"

"Any place conducive to the tone of the film. Erotic. Cutting edge. Heavy on the ambience. I don't know. Read the damn script. That's for you to figure out." He gestured with the cigar again. "Except for one. I've got one location in mind for the bulk of the story, and that's why you're here now."

"What location?" she asked, more confused than ever.

"Greg said you'd be able to get the crew inside to film at Oxygen. If you can do that, you're hired."

A numbing cold swept over her. *"Oxygen?"* Her

voice was little more than a croak. "You want permission to film in the restaurant?"

"You can arrange it, yes? Greg said you know the owner, Kenneth Hooper."

"Harper," she corrected automatically as the room seemed to close in on her. "And yes...I know him."

Miller leaned back in his chair, his arms spread. "Excellent. So you can do it? You'll be my new location scout?"

She swallowed, knowing that the odds of Ken wanting to help her were very, very low. But she was out of options. If she couldn't pull it off, Miller would fire her and she wouldn't be any worse off than she was right then. But if she *could* convince Ken to help her...and if she could find some more locations for Miller...well, if she played her cards right, she could be back on her feet within a year.

"Ms. Neal? An answer today would be good."

She looked up and smiled brightly. "Sorry. Just running through possible locations in my head."

"So you'll do it?"

She held his gaze, careful to keep an expressionless poker face. "On one condition."

He cocked his head. "Condition?"

Her hands trembled, and she held them tight in her lap. "If I pull this off, I want a producer credit. Not associate producer, not line producer. Producer."

For a long moment he said nothing, just stared at her.

"I want my career back, Mr. Miller." Her voice

shook, and she dropped her eyes, sure he was about to tell her to get the hell out of his office.

Leather creaked as he shifted in his chair, and she looked up to see him looking at her quizzically. "Tyrell screwed a lot of people, Ms. Neal. But there were a lot of folks in bed with him who deserved to be screwed. If I do this for you, I'm taking a hell of a risk."

"I wasn't one of the ones who deserved it. I worked my tail off for Tyrell and don't have a damn thing to show for it."

He tapped his thumb against his chin, his mouth turning down into a frown. After a moment he stopped and looked at her, his expression stern. "Ms. Neal?"

She fought a cringe. "Yes?"

"It looks like we have a deal. Don't disappoint me."

"I CAN'T BELIEVE I'm really doing this. I must be a total idiot. It's never going to work. What was I thinking?" Lisa stopped tossing clothes into her suitcase long enough to glare at Greg. "For that matter, what were you thinking?"

Nonplussed, he leaned back against the doorjamb and popped the top on a Dr. Brown's cream soda. "I was thinking you needed the work." He pointed toward her bed and the pile of clothes. "They'll travel better if you fold them."

She was in no mood for packing lessons, and purposefully crumpled her favorite dress and shoved it into her luggage.

"It's your laundry bill."

"I'm not worried about my clothes. I'm worried about this job." She sat on the bed and then flopped backward to stare at the ceiling. "This is a nightmare." Rolling over, she propped herself up on an elbow to look at him. "I'm the last person Ken's going to want to help."

"The man's going to jump through hoops to help you. You were the love of his life."

She cringed, knowing all too well how much she'd hurt him. "'Were' being the operative word." Her eyes welled, and she flashed a weak smile at Greg. "I'm thirsty," she lied. "Would you get me a soda?"

He nodded, probably knowing she needed privacy more than she needed a drink, and slipped out toward the kitchen.

With a sigh, she rolled over, dragging her pillow across her face. She'd made a huge mistake hitching her star to Drake Tyrell, and made an even bigger mistake leaving Los Angeles in the first place.

She'd been so naive. Working for Drake had been the biggest thrill of her life, and she'd actually seen two movies come out with her name as associate producer...before her world had come crashing down.

At the time she'd smelled success, so she'd thrown herself even more into the work, giving it every ounce of energy she had, knowing there'd be nothing left for a personal life, especially not a personal life an entire continent away. She'd had her eye on the prize, so she'd sucked up her courage and told Ken she wanted some time apart and unattached.

She didn't regret the decision. Not then, not now. But she'd always regretted the consequences of that decision. She'd hurt Ken, and she'd never really told him how sorry she was.

After the breakup, Tyrell had told her that her sacrifices were worth it because she was going to be a real player someday. Lousy, lying bastard.

He hadn't meant a word of it—he'd just wanted Lisa in his bed and, by the end of a year, that's exactly where she was. Ken found out, of course, since the affair was plastered all over the tabloids. Even though they'd already broken up, Lisa's sleeping with Tyrell had hurt Ken—badly—and she hated herself for it.

When the studio shut them down and Tyrell fled for his native Britain, Lisa was out on her own—and her production credits didn't mean a thing. She had a scarlet T on her forehead, and it was all she could do to find work on even the lowest-budget flicks.

Greg came back in, jarring her from her thoughts, and she sat up in time to see him flip the desk chair around to straddle. He crossed his arms over the backrest and nodded toward the diet Coke can on her nightstand. "Feeling better?"

"You're just too damn perceptive."

"I know. It's a gift."

"I feel fine." She took a sip, letting the fizzy drink work its magic. "I'm not going to be royally humiliated until later when I'm in Los Angeles."

"If you don't think you have a chance, why'd you take the job?"

"Because I'm an idiot." She scooted backward and slipped off the bed to start packing again, this time taking more care to fold each item. After a second she sighed and looked him in the eye. "Okay. You win. I took it because it's the best shot I've had in a long time."

"You're welcome."

"You just want me in L.A. so you can have the bedroom."

"True enough."

He laughed, but she knew he was only half joking. They shared the one-bedroom apartment with two others, a flight attendant and another actor/waiter. Each month, one of them got dibs on the bedroom and the others shared the living room with its three foam chairs that pulled out into tiny beds. So much for pop culture's perception about life in the big city. Monica and Rachel might have their own bedrooms and a humongous apartment, but *Friends* was a far cry from Lisa's reality.

"You okay?" he asked.

She nodded, realizing she was biting her lower lip. "Yeah. Just nervous. If I can pull off the locations, I'll get a producer credit." She looked him in the eye. "And if the film does well, that means my career will be back on track. I've got a lot riding on this job, and for all I know Ken's just going to slam the door in my face."

"Then you won't be any worse off than you are

now.'' He moved to sit on the bed. ''But I think you're going to do great.''

Her smile felt watery. ''Thanks. I appreciate you going out on a limb for me. Really.''

''What can I say? I'm a heck of a guy.''

''You?'' she teased. ''I hadn't noticed.''

His grin widened. ''No? You should pay more attention.''

At that, she laughed outright then her smile faded to a frown again. ''I'm just afraid Ken's going to laugh in my face. And I wouldn't blame him one bit. I was a bitch. Self-centered and stupid.''

''Ah, but now you're a reformed bitch. Or at least you're a charter member of Bitches Anonymous and firmly on the wagon.''

She managed a smile, wondering if it was true. If it came down to it, would she do the same thing all over again?

''Seriously,'' he continued, ''there's no crime in wanting to focus on your career.''

''I know. But I'm sure he thinks I left him for Tyrell, not for Tyrell's job offer.'' She sighed. ''Besides, fat lot of good it did me. I came out here expecting to return to L.A. in triumph, and look at me. I'm going back now with less in my checking account than when I was fresh out of school.''

''I don't think Ken's going to care about your checkbook.''

''Except to feel some smug satisfaction that I blew it.''

Greg's smile was patient. Clearly he knew she was

in one of her moods. "The way you've described him, I don't think he's the holier-than-thou type."

She wasn't ready to concede. "Maybe not five years ago, but he's Mr. Big Shot now."

"And a damn good-looking Mr. Big Shot, too," Greg said.

"He's not your type." She smiled, but her heart wasn't in it.

"Too bad."

"Do you know I went to the opening of Oxygen? That was the night he was going to ask me to marry him. Of course, I found that out later, after I told him I was moving back to New York. Not a very happy memory, and now I'm supposed to go back and ask to film there? Do you have any idea how many old wounds this is going to open?"

"So don't take the job."

"Ha, ha." Taking a fortifying breath, she latched her suitcase and tugged it off the bed. "Wish me luck. I'm off to beg a favor from my ex-boyfriend."

"Good luck."

She paused in the doorway. "Thanks. I'm going to need it."

3

"THANKS for choosing the Bellisimo, Ms. Neal. Enjoy your stay."

Through a haze of exhaustion, Lisa thanked the clerk as she clutched her room key, still not quite believing that Avenue F was footing the bill for her to stay in a hotel as lush as the Bellisimo. She hadn't slept at all the night before, and now she was having trouble remembering her name, much less what she did with her luggage. She looked down toward her ankles, trying to find the matched set of suitcases her mother had given her years ago and fought a wave of panic until she remembered the bellhop had taken them.

Stifling a yawn, she surveyed the lobby, trying to find the bellman and her bags. The hotel was just as she'd remembered it. Polished marble columns, polished hardwood floor, everything shiny and gleaming and not the least bit understated. The place practically smelled of money, and it attracted the type of clientele who were drawn to that particular scent.

Exactly the kind of atmosphere Ken had wanted for his very first restaurant—a prestigious address with a crowd made up of climbers and those already at the top. As Lisa glanced around, she knew he had to be pleased. Not some small part of his success was tied to his skill in choosing the right location.

Some sort of convention was going on, and the lobby was filled to overflowing with men and women in suits sporting little plastic name tags. When the crowd finally parted a bit, Lisa caught a glimpse of the bellhop near the bank of elevators. With a wave, she signaled that she was on her way.

Actually getting to him was a bit more tricky, and she ended up having to squeeze between the stacks of luggage left lying around by the conventioneers, a process that took a lot more energy than she had left. She finally made it, though she ended up feeling frazzled and far too jostled for comfort.

After handing the bellhop her room key, she ran her hands through her hair, sure she was probably making it a spiky mess. Not that it mattered. The one thing she wanted was to get to her room, then collapse on her bed for a long nap and spend a few blissful hours completely ignoring the problem that had kept her awake in the first place—how she was going to persuade Ken Harper to help her.

The bellhop punched the elevator button, and Lisa leaned against the cool marble wall as they waited for a car to arrive. In truth, persuading Ken wasn't her biggest worry. No, what she feared most was her reaction—and his—when she saw him again.

When she'd told Ken she was leaving five years ago, she had no way of knowing that he'd been planning to ask her to marry him that very night. She'd found out the next day when she'd gone to the restaurant to say goodbye to Tim and Chris and all the other friends she'd made. Tim's usually cheerful face had seemed cold and closed off, and she'd pushed him to tell her what was wrong.

When he told her about Ken's plans, she'd gone cold inside, but she hadn't changed her mind. Ken had wanted to wait until marriage to sleep together, but Lisa'd never made any promises. If anything, she'd been completely forthright. Marriage wasn't on her radar—then or now. Five years ago she'd been entirely focused on her career. Her whole life she'd wanted a career in the film industry, and she'd had no intentions of getting distracted by a relationship. Maybe someday she'd marry and have a family, but not now—and certainly not back when she'd moved to New York.

Not that leaving had been easy. She adored Ken. Maybe they hadn't slept together, but his kisses, his touch, *his nearness* had always done amazing things to her body, making her breathless and tingly in a way no man since had ever made her feel. He had always been a perfect gentleman—had never teased her sexually and then pulled away. And despite the firm boundaries in their relationship, there'd been a chemistry between them that was undeniable.

She'd wanted to sleep with him, had wanted him to gather her in his arms and make love to her for long, endless nights—but she'd fought the feeling, using all her effort to box that passion and push it to a secluded corner of her mind.

In a weird way, Ken's old-fashioned insistence saved her. Her reaction to him was explosive, and she wasn't sure she would have been able to keep her focus if they'd given in to passion.

The bell sounding the arrival of the elevator pulled her from her thoughts, and she stifled a shiver. Now that she was here, she was terrified that she'd react just as powerfully to Ken—but that he'd only react to her with anger and hurt.

"After you, miss." The bellhop held open the door, gesturing for her to enter the windowed elevator. He followed with his cart laden with her luggage, and a swarm of conventioneers piled in after him, pushing her all the way to the back. A wave of claustrophobia swept over her, and she turned around to look through the glass at the lobby coffee shop, trying to ignore the uncomfortable press of people behind her.

Her gaze swept the lounge, taking in the chic attire of the Los Angeles elite. Still early morning, and already the movers and shakers were having their breakfast meetings, making decisions. Producers were meeting with directors, agents were meeting with actors, and more than anything, she wanted to be in on the action.

With a little sigh, she pressed her forehead to the glass and was just about to close her eyes when a familiar movement caught her eye. She blinked, trying to figure out what she'd seen.

And then there it was again—a starched white shirt, khakis, broad shoulders, a head of thick brown hair.

He moved with the casualness of the completely self-confident.

Her pulse quickened. Even from behind, she knew that body, knew the way those broad shoulders moved as he walked, knew the way those strong thighs felt beneath her fingers.

The elevator stopped and most of the convention-eers stepped off. She knew she should move away from the glass, quit watching before he turned around. But she couldn't tear herself away. He was following a hostess to a table near a potted palm, and when they arrived, he pulled out his chair and turned around to sit, facing her.

From her angle above him she couldn't see his entire face, but what she could see made her stomach twist with memories, both delightful and disturbing. Slowly, almost as if he felt her watching, he lifted his head and seemed to look right at her.

She gasped and took an involuntary step back, banging into the bellhop's cart and almost tripping.

"Are you okay, miss?"

"What?" She was still staring at the glass, trying to work up the courage to step closer to see if he was still looking up at her. "Oh. Yes. I'm fine. Just tired. Long plane ride."

"Well, you'll have a room and a comfortable bed soon."

She nodded vaguely as she gripped the handrail, her fingers tight against the brass bar. Trying for casual, she stepped toward the glass and peered through it to the lounge below. Their eyes met, and her body tingled from a rush of warmth that spread through her, languid and inviting. She held his gaze until, finally, the elevator rose high enough that she could no longer see him.

She exhaled, her breath shaky. She had no idea if he'd really seen her, or if he'd just been looking in her direction. Even if he had seen the woman in the elevator, would he recognize her after five years? She didn't know.

She gnawed her lower lip, knowing one thing for certain—at least on her part, whatever chemistry, whatever magic, had been between them five years ago, was just as overwhelming today.

IT COULDN'T HAVE BEEN HER. Absolutely not. No way.

He'd been repeating the mantra for more than ten hours, ever since he'd noticed the woman rising in the elevator. The woman with the slim figure and the chin-length blond hair. The woman he imagined was Lisa.

Not possible. And not worth obsessing about.

He needed to quit obsessing and to focus on his work. He'd left the hotel right after breakfast to run the gauntlet between his clubs and restaurants in Orange County, Ventura and Palm Springs. He'd crawled back to Oxygen at midnight and the restaurant was now hopping with late-night energy. Though the dinner crowd had left, the place was by no means empty. A few late diners dotted the tables, along with folks who'd come in for dessert and coffee. In the lounge area, a small crowd had already gathered on the dance floor as the jazz band cranked out favorites from the thirties and forties.

Ken eased his way from the main dining area to the lounge, trying to focus his thoughts. They focused all right—directly on the woman in the elevator. There'd been something about the way she'd looked at him, something about the way she'd held herself. And he'd been unable to rip his eyes away.

Frustrated, he took a seat at the bar, then tugged at his tie, loosening the blasted thing.

"Something on your mind, boss?" Chris put down a napkin, then topped it with a tall glass of sparkling water.

"Just thinking about old times."

"Not surprised. Coming up on five years. That's a hell of an accomplishment."

True enough, but what Ken was thinking about wasn't his restaurant; it was his ex-girlfriend. Still, he didn't intend to clue his bartender in on this particular neurosis, and he lifted the glass in a toast. "To five more years."

Chris nodded. "I'll drink to that."

"Not on the job you won't," he said in a jokingly stern tone.

"Whatever you say, boss," he said, grinning as he turned to help one of the guests.

Ken swiveled on his stool, surveying the restaurant he'd started on a shoestring five years ago. No wonder he'd had such a visceral reaction to the woman in the elevator. Five years ago Lisa had walked out. In one week he'd face the anniversary of both her departure and his grand opening. Who wouldn't be a little raw? And it was certainly no surprise that he was seeing ghosts in the elevators.

But that's all she was—a ghost. Ken needed to forget Lisa and to move on with his life. Not that he was interested in jumping back into the dating game. What he'd told Tim was true. If the right woman came along, great. But he had no intention of searching her out. Considering he had to hire someone to run his clothes to the dry cleaner's and pick up his groceries, he had no time to waste looking for a date.

Once upon a time he might have been craving the domestic life, but no more. He'd made a success of himself, and he had everything he could possibly want. Everything. He didn't need to go hunting up trouble.

He was practicing not thinking about Lisa, or the woman in the elevator, or women in general, when the maître d', Charles, caught his eye, signaling for him to come over. A woman was standing next to Charles, her face obscured by the ornate columns near the entrance. Since Charles tended to be protective of Ken's time, if he thought it was important for Ken to meet her, chances were she was a celebrity, a restaurant critic or some other mover and shaker in the Hollywood scene.

His professional demeanor in place, he moved toward the front of the restaurant. As he drew near, he realized who the woman was, but by then it was too late to turn back gracefully. Instead, he steeled himself and headed forward.

Alicia Duncan turned as he approached, her television-ready smile gleaming. "Ken!" She held out a hand for him to take. "Kiss, kiss! It's so wonderful to see you again."

"Alicia." He took a fortifying breath. As usual, she looked so picture-perfect it was scary. In the two years he'd known her, Ken didn't think he'd ever seen her without every hair in place and her makeup just so—even during some of their more intimate moments.

He clasped her hand in his, and let go as quickly as etiquette allowed. "What a nice surprise." He was in no mood to hear Alicia's pitch again, and he said a silent prayer that maybe she really had come only for a late dinner.

"I was hoping to catch you." She leaned in closer and he could smell bourbon on her breath. A lot of bourbon. "I need to talk to you. A favor."

"Alicia—"

She held up a hand. "Dammit, Kenny. Just five minutes? Can't you spare me five minutes of your precious time?"

He cringed at the nickname, but nodded. "Five minutes."

Not worrying about being polite, he grasped her elbow, led her to the kitchen, then parked them just inside the swinging doors. His back was to the dining room, but he'd stepped far enough in to be out of the staff's traffic. Tim looked up for a moment, clearly curious but too preoccupied to pay much attention. The rest of the staff was too busy even to take notice.

"What?" he said without preamble.

She jumped slightly, her mouth set in a little pout. "Kenny, I'm surprised. I just want to talk and you're being so..." Her hand twirled as she searched for a word. "So short."

"I'm not being short," he said, knowing he was. "I just don't see the point in repeating what Marty already told you. I don't want to do a talk show. It's not my style, and you know it."

Was it his imagination, or did her smile seem menacing? "I just want you to reconsider."

"It's nothing personal, Alicia." He tried to keep his voice pleasant.

She moved closer, her smile shifting from cold to seductive, and he fought a chill. "It's always personal," she purred as she closed the distance between them.

"Don't." He took a deep breath. "Look, Alicia, you know talk shows aren't my style."

"Then do it for me," she whispered as one thin arm snaked up around his neck. She looked him in the eyes. "You dumped me, remember?" she whispered. "Don't you think you owe me?"

He felt his features automatically freeze into place. At one time he'd felt some attraction for this woman—enough to go out with her, anyway—but not anymore, and now it just pissed him off that she was trying to play the sex kitten to get what she wanted. Especially when he'd already said no.

"Alicia..." He tried to pull away, but she only moved closer.

"For old times' sake," she said, even as she pressed her body against his. In one practiced movement she was up on her toes, her lips pressed to his. She was a beautiful woman, not half bad in bed, and he felt absolutely nothing—not a twinge, not a spark, not anything—nothing except some vague semblance of pity that she'd stoop to throwing herself at him.

Gently, he pushed her away even as a little voice in the back of his mind urged him to just do the damn show. After all, it wouldn't kill him, and she must really be in a bind if she was that desperate. But he didn't intend to compromise his principles. Not for Alicia, not for anybody.

"Go home, Alicia."

She clung to him, the bourbon clearly getting the better of her, as he maneuvered them toward the swinging doors. He almost tripped over her feet, but finally managed to get her steady.

When he looked up, he almost dropped her again.

There, standing right in front of him, was the love of his life. The woman he'd wanted to marry. The woman who'd walked out on him. The woman who made his blood boil.

The woman he needed to forget.

A tiny smile graced her beautiful mouth. "Hi, Ken," Lisa said. "I was hoping you'd have a minute to talk."

LISA WATCHED as a flurry of emotions passed over his face. More tersely than she would have anticipated, he said goodbye to the woman named Alicia. Then he turned to her, his face devoid of emotion, and steered her toward a secluded table. The pressure of his fingers on the small of her back sent a once-familiar chill racing down her spine as they moved through the near-deserted restaurant.

Oxygen had changed very little in the past five years. It still had that air of quiet elegance that Ken had worked so hard for, and she let her gaze drift over the few remaining guests as Ken led her through the room.

Although a part of her dreaded having to explain why she needed help, for the most part, Lisa was proud of the way she'd kept her voice steady despite the shock of seeing Ken with another woman surgically attached to his lips.

She'd known it would be hard seeing him face-to-face after so much time, but what she hadn't expected were the stabbing needles of jealousy she'd felt when a waiter had pushed open the swinging doors and she'd caught a glimpse of their embrace. And that jealousy made her more than a little uncomfortable. She was here for a job, not to strike up a relationship. It had been five years. Whatever had once been between them was long over. He could kiss whomever he wanted whenever he wanted. It really wasn't any of her business.

Still, she had to admit to feeling a small sense of satisfaction when his eyes had widened and his mouth had opened. She'd never forgotten him, not one detail, but she'd always feared that somehow he'd managed to put her out of his head, that he wouldn't recognize her if he saw her again.

He'd recognized her, all right. And there was no hiding the white-hot anger mixed with desire that clouded his eyes. She'd seen it, plain as day, and her stomach had clenched from the knowledge that she'd hurt him so badly the pain was still raw.

That look was gone now. He'd erased it in an instant before sending the woman he'd kissed on her way. And now, as they arrived at a table by a window overlooking Sunset Boulevard, he was nothing more than coldly professional.

"Have a seat." Ice dripped from his voice. He pulled out her chair, then sat opposite her across the table, the hard angles of his face seeming more stern and foreboding in the flickering candlelight.

She licked her lips, trying to cure a severe case of cotton mouth. She saw him focus on the movement, a hint of desire flashing in the deep blue irises, and she relaxed a tiny bit. Maybe he wasn't as good at turning off his emotions as he liked to pretend.

Almost as if realizing he'd revealed something of himself, he ripped his gaze away, then roughly pulled back his sleeve to reveal his watch. "I've got fifteen minutes before I say good-night to the last guests." He paused, his eyes meeting hers, and this time they reflected only annoyance. "Why are you here, Lisa?"

She flinched at the harshness in his voice, but didn't let him rattle her. Of course he was going to be upset. But she needed his help, and that meant she had to stay calm and reasonable.

"Lisa?" he repeated as she counted to ten. "What do you want?"

What did she want? Well, that was the question of the hour. Fame, fortune, to right past mistakes, to rebuild burned bridges. But there was no easy way to say all of that, and in the end she simply said, "Help. I need your help."

"My help?" His forehead creased as he leaned back in his chair, regarding her, an unfamiliar coldness in his eyes. "All this time, and you walk back through the door and announce you need *my* help?"

She nodded, her eyes burning with the effort to hold back tears. Part of her wanted to throw her arms around him and tell him she was sorry for the hurt, sorry for being so focused on her career, and to beg him to tell her all was forgiven.

But that was a selfish dream. For one thing, while she'd never meant to hurt him, the truth was that she'd done what she needed to do, and she'd do it all over if she had to. She had to get her career off the ground. *She had to.* Five years ago, that meant leaving him. Today, it meant begging him for help.

"Why, Lisa?" he asked, his voice thick with emotion. "Why should I help you?"

She couldn't stop the single tear that escaped, tracing a path down her cheek. "Because once, a long time ago, you told me you loved me."

4

"I DID LOVE YOU." He struggled to not let his voice betray him, because if he was honest with himself he probably loved her still. Loved her, hated her, and everything in between.

Every emotion had gathered into a tight knot in his gut, and it was all he could do to keep his voice steady, to hold on to the control he worked so hard to maintain.

Lord knows, no other woman had ever affected him as much, had ever gotten under his skin the way she had. Passion, lust...love? He didn't know. All he knew was that she'd poisoned him, infected his blood, shaken his self-control—and that was what had really thrown him for a loop.

She seemed to shrink away, probably in part from the dry, emotionless tone of his voice. But that was the only option—either no emotion, or let loose with every emotion that was raging within him. He'd opened himself once to Lisa Neal. He wasn't the kind of man who made the same mistake twice.

"Will you help me?" Her voice was small, pleading, and he had to wonder what was so important that she would come to him after so many years.

If he were a stronger man, he'd tell her to go away. He'd tell her that five years ago he would have done anything for her, but that now he had no interest in helping her, no reason to help her.

But, dammit, he wasn't that strong. And he was curious to know what twist of fate had brought her back to him after so much time. After caring so little that she could simply walk away, what now spurred her to gather her pride and come knocking at his door?

He signaled for Chris to bring them a bottle of wine, then leaned back in his chair, his arms crossed over his chest. "What is it you want me to do?"

Relief flashed in her eyes, but she was smart enough to know she wasn't home free yet. She pressed her lips together, then folded her hands primly on the tabletop. Chris slipped over, dropping off an uncorked bottle of a Napa cabernet and two glasses before drifting back into the shadows. Lisa eyed the bottle, so Ken poured her a glass, sliding it to her side of the table.

She gulped it, downing half the glass in one swallow, then took a deep breath before meeting his eyes again. "Things didn't work out in New York," she said.

The fury he'd been containing bubbled to the surface, his head filling with noise as blood pounded in his ears. "So, since things didn't work out with Tyrell, you're rushing back to me?" He spat out the words, not even trying for civility.

For a moment she looked shocked, then she

reached down to pick up her purse. "I'm sorry." She stood. "I shouldn't have come. I don't know what I was thinking."

For just an instant he considered letting her walk away, letting her leave his life again—and maybe this time she'd leave his heart, too. But he couldn't do it. He caught her arm as she moved past him.

"Let go."

"Lisa," he whispered, and damned if his voice didn't hitch. "I'm sorry." He nodded toward the table. "Please. Sit down."

She hesitated only a second before slipping back into her chair. This time she didn't look at him, and instead concentrated on her wineglass. "Like I said, my plans in New York didn't work out."

"But I saw the trades. I even watched a few movies that you'd worked on with…him." He couldn't bring himself to say Tyrell's name.

She looked up, her eyes misty. "You watched my movies?"

His heart twisted, but he tamped down the tug of emotion, needing to stay clearheaded.

She didn't wait for him to answer. "You must not have followed my career after that."

That much was true. He'd been so infuriated that she and Tyrell had become a couple, that he'd quit paying attention, deciding that he'd simply been torturing himself by paying any attention at all.

"Let's just say I wasn't able to parlay my work on those movies into anything else after Tyrell's production company bottomed out." Despite the flat tone, she couldn't hide the sadness in her voice.

An intense urge to take her hand, to soothe, caught him by surprise, and he fought to keep some distance. She'd hurt him, and it would take more than conciliatory words to make amends. "So what have you been doing?"

"This and that. Nothing like what I'd planned, that's for sure." Her mouth curved up into an ironic smile. "Lately, I've been doing temp work." She took a breath. "Until now, anyway. Now I've got a real shot again. A decent break."

"And you need my help." His words were sharp, his tone cutting.

She nodded, just one curt movement of her head.

"Even if I wanted to help you, I'm not exactly involved in the film scene. What could I possibly do?"

"Winston Miller is shooting a sequel to *The Velvet Bed* in Los Angeles. I'm his location scout. It's my job to find a dozen or so super-sexy locations around Los Angeles to film at." She shrugged. "Not the greatest job, but if I nail it, Miller's offered me a producer credit."

"Which is exactly what you always wanted to do."

She rolled her eyes. "Right. Except I wanted to work at a studio. But any producer credit now will get my foot in the door. And it'll get me back to Los Angeles. Back to the heart of the industry."

"So what do you need me for?"

She licked her lips. "The restaurant. Oxygen. Miller wants to film here."

He balked. Not so much at the request, but at his almost immediate, unexpected reaction to open the doors for her. He'd never allowed a film crew on site. *Never*. And just moments ago he'd turned Alica down flat when she'd made essentially the same request.

"I know it's asking a lot..." She trailed off, the tip of her finger tracing a pattern on the wineglass.

"It is." Disconcerted, he stood, ran a hand through his hair. "I have to go get ready for closing. Meet me tomorrow. Breakfast. Hugo's at nine."

He hadn't meant to meet her eyes, but he couldn't help it, and when he did, he saw that they were wide and full of hope—hope he'd put there. And damned if he didn't like the feeling.

"You'll help me?"

"I'll think about it."

"Thank you."

As if she knew the moment was tenuous, she stood quickly and kissed him lightly on the cheek before slipping past him.

"Don't thank me yet," he whispered, even though she'd gone. He didn't have a clue what the hell he was doing or why he was doing it. And he wasn't inclined to examine his motives right then.

One thing, though, was certain—his motives were anything but pure.

HE WAS DRUNK, and it felt nice. The liquor had dulled the pain of seeing her again, of knowing she was there because of what he could do for her, not because she wanted to see him. The knowledge made him feel raw, especially since every atom in his body still wanted her. Despite the fresh waves of hurt and anger that washed over him when he thought of her, the bottom line was, he wanted Lisa in his bed. He always had.

But he'd lost that chance years ago. She'd probably thought of him as some sort of country bumpkin, out of place among the L.A. power players. She'd supported his dream, but she'd never really believed he'd be one of them. Not a player. Not as she intended to be. And in the end that meant she needed a man other than Ken. A man like Tyrell who could help her get where she wanted to be. Ken may have been an enjoyable dalliance, but he wasn't permanent material, not for someone like Lisa.

Disgusted with himself for dredging up old hurts and insecurities, he tossed back the contents of his glass, letting the slow burn of whiskey eat away at his despair.

"You should slow down," Tim warned, even as he topped off Ken's drink. The restaurant was closed and dark, but Tim had stayed around, apparently sensing an aberration in his friend's usually predictable life.

"I don't have to drive home." Ken tipped the glass back, took a long swallow. "Keep it coming."

Four years ago it had seemed easier just to move into the hotel. His dreams of having some sort of home life had crumbled around him, and the hotel had the advantage of built-in maid service, easy access to work, the constant thrum of activity to ward off loneliness. The perfect living arrangements. At least, that's what he told himself.

"I'm going to pull the plug soon. You're so trashed you'll get cited for a D.U.I. in the elevator."

"This is twice now she's done this," he said, his fingers tightening on the glass as he ignored Tim's comment.

"Who's done what?"

"Lisa. Used me as a damn stepping stone."

Tim poured himself a shot of bourbon and sat across from Ken. His boss's mind tended to go a mile a minute anyway, so Ken was always at least two steps ahead of everyone else. Usually, though, Tim could catch up pretty quick. Tonight, he was lost. "Come again?"

"Five years ago I was the romantic interlude on her journey to find a lover who could help her career. Now she's back, and—surprise, surprise—it's all about her job again."

Tim took a long swallow, trying to decide what to say. He'd known Ken for seven years, and Lisa for almost six. He'd spent countless hours with the two of them, heard them laughing and teasing as they painted the restaurant or poured over plans. He'd seen the way she'd begged a blanket from housekeeping when the late hours got to Ken and he fell asleep behind the unvarnished bar.

No woman could tuck a man in so gently, with such a soft look on her face, and not feel real, deep emotions. Lisa'd loved Ken, all right. But that didn't change the fact that she'd left, and now Tim didn't know what to say, didn't know how to help ease the pain.

He decided to not say anything, just simply asked, "What does she want?"

"To film inside the restaurant."

"Whoa!" Tim knew better than anyone how Ken felt about keeping a mystique surrounding Oxygen. "What are you going to do?"

"I'm not sure."

Tim frowned. He'd expected a rousing refusal. No one filmed inside the restaurant, and that included ex-girlfriends and objects of obsession. That Ken was even considering the possibility was not only a bit unnerving, it was also very, very interesting.

Ken picked up his glass and swirled the liquid, watching as the melting ice clattered against the sides of the tumbler. The liquor had fogged his head, true, but not so much that he didn't know exactly what he was doing. "I'm thinking of a little tit for tat."

The plan was forming even as he spoke the words. Decadent, yes, but extremely appealing.

"What do you mean?" Tim asked. "You're going to let them film here?"

"Possibly. She wants to use me. Maybe I want to use her, too." Hell, maybe he *needed* to use her. Maybe that was the only way to set the past aside.

With a clarity he was used to experiencing only in his business deals, the plan came to him full-blown.

Since Lisa, he'd had his share of women, but not one had satisfied the hole she'd left in his heart. He'd loved her, true. But he was long past love. He had to be. Any emotion left was just residual and, more than anything, he needed her out of his system, needed to break through the red wall of anger pressing up against him.

But he also wanted her.

Lust and revenge, a potent combination.

Potent enough to throw his principles out the window? Potent enough to let her into Oxygen?

He ran his hands over his face, remembering all those nights when he'd longed to sink himself into her. He'd held back then, so sure that one day she'd be his wife. Well, he'd lost then. She'd walked out, leaving him with nothing but memories and an ache in his heart.

He didn't intend to lose now. So help him, he wanted her.

Tim was watching him, disbelief in his eyes. "You're not thinking what I think you're thinking?"

Ken half smiled, knowing Tim would disapprove. "Since I can't read minds, I couldn't say."

Tim shook his head. "Be careful, buddy."

"I'm always careful," Ken said, slamming back the rest of his drink.

"You need coffee. You're not thinking clearly."

"On the contrary, this is the most focused I've been since I started thinking about the anniversary." He moved toward the door, only slightly unsteady on his feet. "Lock up when you leave," he called, even though he knew Tim would.

He headed for the elevator, planning to hit the sheets immediately. But when his alarm went off the next morning, he realized he had no memory of getting from the restaurant to his suite, much less getting into bed. Since he was still wearing his suit, he apparently hadn't put too much thought into the endeavor.

With a groan, he sat up, one hand pressed against his temple to keep his brain from spilling out his ears. He almost called the front desk to have them stop the damn construction, until he realized the pounding was all in his head.

Memories of the night before flickered through his mind, scattered and indistinct. *Lisa.* Lisa was the only impression that stood out. The only real memory in a haze of illusions. Lisa…and his plan.

Stumbling into the bathroom, he pressed his hands against the counter and stared at the mirror. His reflection stared back, stern and unblinking. Could he really do this? Did he still want her so much—and did he want retribution so much—that he was willing to make sex a bargaining tool? That he was willing to sacrifice his hard-and-fast rule against filming inside the restaurant?

He took a deep breath. Anger or lust, he didn't know, it didn't matter. The answer was still the same—*yes.*

Ken shut his eyes against his reflection's reproach. Lord help him, yes.

HUGO'S was just as she'd remembered it. A popular breakfast spot on Santa Monica Boulevard in the heart of West Hollywood, it was a favorite hangout among gays and straights, the trendy and the hungry. When she'd lived there, it had been Lisa's favorite place to grab a weekend breakfast, and she'd become addicted to the pumpkin pancakes.

Her stomach was already growling as she pulled into a parking space behind the restaurant. She sat in her rental car for a moment, gathering her courage. This was it. In an hour, she'd either have Ken's help or she wouldn't.

And if he turned her down, she didn't have a clue what she was going to do. Maybe pick up a copy of *Daily Variety* to see if she could find a job doing grunt work on a low-budget film.

No! She pounded her fist against the steering wheel, then quickly looked around to see if anyone had noticed the whacked-out woman in the blue Honda. She needed this job, was terrified of failing once again, and she was going to convince Ken to help her—no matter what the cost.

With a deep breath, she slid out of the car, then started walking toward the front entrance. A dozen or so people loitered near the door, newspapers in hand, as they waited for the hostess to take them to a table. The inside wasn't any better. The crowd was so thick, Lisa could barely fight her way to the hostess station.

"I'm sorry," the hostess said after Lisa explained she was meeting a friend. "We're only seating full parties right now. If you don't see your friend, you're probably here first.'' She poised a pencil above a yellow pad. "Name?"

"Neal," Lisa said. With a sigh, she slipped away, then leaned against the wall. She'd intentionally showed up a little late so she wouldn't seem overly eager. So much for that little scheme, since Ken wasn't even there yet.

A warm hand closed over her shoulder. "Lisa," Ken said.

A bone-deep warmth flowed through her, and she trembled. His voice alone made her pulse burn, igniting long-forgotten passions that she had absolutely no business letting rekindle. She was over him. They were history. And she'd do well to remember that.

She turned to face him, hoping her smile was professional, and that it didn't betray the riot of emotions raging inside her. "I didn't realize you were here," she said. "We should tell the hostess. The wait's forever."

His self-assured grin was devilish. "Not a problem." He took her arm and steered her into the dining area, neatly passing the hostess, who didn't even give them a second glance.

When he slowed in front of a not-yet-cleared table with coffee, orange juice, a half-eaten croissant and a folded newspaper, Lisa dug in her heels.

"Problem?"

"You're just going to grab some dirty table?"

He pulled out a chair and motioned her to sit down. "*Our* dirty table."

"Our..." She blinked. "Of course. The fabulous

Ken Harper doesn't have to follow the rules. He gets seated even before his entire party arrives.''

"Professional courtesy. I'm a regular. Plus, I've been here for an hour.''

"An hour." She quirked a brow. "You must have been anxious to see me.''

"I was. I am." He smiled, and her insides twitched in response.

As soon as he was seated, the waitress glided over in a fit of extreme efficiency. Starving, Lisa ordered the pumpkin pancakes and a latte. She waited for the waitress to disappear out of earshot before facing Ken directly across the table.

"Well?" Silverware clattered as she released it from the napkin. She twisted the cloth in her lap. "Have you thought about what I asked?''

His eyes seemed to bore into hers. "Oh, yes. I thought about it." His eyes softened, and she fidgeted under his steady gaze. "That's about all I did last night." His eyes roamed over her face, a silent caress, until his eyes met hers again. "I just thought about it.''

She looked away, thrown off-balance by the feeling that he'd been thinking not only about her proposal, but about *her*. And even more disconcerted to realize she liked the feeling. "So, um, what did you decide?''

In her lap, she crossed her fingers. Tight. And she held her breath.

"I decided it wasn't quite a fair trade.''

Resisting the urge to close her eyes, she slowly

exhaled. "A trade? I—I don't understand. I asked for a favor."

"I know you did. But I didn't get where I am today by giving away something for nothing." He draped one arm over the back of his chair and took a sip of orange juice. The morning light streaming in through the window glistened in his rich brown hair, and he looked perfectly at ease. A Los Angeles version of an Olympian god, totally male, totally powerful. Totally sexy.

With some effort, she got her wandering thoughts under control. What the hell was she doing there? And what the devil had possessed her to come crawling back to Ken Harper? She was in over her head.

"I'm talking about quid pro quo," he said, then smiled, the image of a man completely comfortable with his place in the world.

She swallowed. Way, way over her head.

"Understand?" he asked.

"Of course." She spoke calmly as her mind raced. She didn't have one damn thing to bargain with. Winston hadn't given her a budget, so she couldn't offer Ken money. He'd get a film credit, but if he wasn't interested in filming in his restaurant, the enticement value of a credit was probably nil. Basically, she had bupkiss—which, of course, he knew.

"You know I don't like that kind of cheap publicity, so at first I considered just saying no."

"At first?"

He shrugged, took a sip of orange juice. "I could tell this was important to you."

"It is," she whispered, suddenly sure he was going to help her. The question was, what would it cost her?

He nodded. "So I thought, what's the one thing I've always wanted, but never had?" His voice rolled over her, low and dangerous. The voice of a man she didn't know—had *never* known. She ran her teeth over her lower lip, wondering if she'd made a mistake, but knowing that she had to stick it out, no matter what.

He leaned in, close enough that she could feel his breath against her skin and smell the musky scent of his cologne. The hairs on the back of her neck popped up, and she fought the urge to look away.

"I asked myself, what's the one thing Lisa can get for me if I do her this favor?"

She knew the look in his eyes, she'd seen it before, years ago…on nights when he'd come within a hairbreadth of breaking his own vow to not sleep with her unless they were married. It was a look she used to cherish. Now it scared her, made her wonder if she shouldn't catch the next plane back to New York.

Slowly she shook her head. "I don't have anything to offer, Ken. I'm sorry, but I don't."

"Yes, you do, sweetheart."

She licked her lips, afraid she knew the answer even before she asked the question. "What, Ken? What have I got to offer?"

His smile just about stopped her heart. "You. You want my restaurant. I want you."

5

"ME?" HER VOICE SQUEAKED, so she tried again. "You want me?" Oh, Lord. It was exactly what she'd imagined, but until he'd said it, she hadn't really believed it. And now, faced with the proposition, she wondered if she could agree. For years she'd told herself she was over him. But if she...if they...

She'd always wondered what it would be like to make love to Ken. But not now. Not when there was nothing left between them but memories and hurt—a hurt she'd caused.

"Lisa?"

The trouble was, the attraction was still there...and that made the offer damned enticing. Licking her lips, she regarded him. "Sex? We're talking about sex?"

He chuckled. "Say it a little louder. I don't think they heard you in the back of the restaurant."

She sat up straighter, trying to hold on to her dignity. "I, uh, just want to be clear on what it is we're negotiating." Her logical side knew she should be indignant, even angry. But somehow the anger wasn't there. Instead there was just a hollow feeling in her stomach that she recognized as guilt. She'd hurt him. Now he wanted her to pay.

The corner of his mouth curved as he leaned forward to take her hand. The warmth of his skin enticed, and she couldn't deny the little surge of adrenaline that shot through her simply because of the physical contact. Disconcerted, she tried to pull her hand away, but he held fast, not answering, but also not letting go. Instead he was just looking at her in a way that suggested he could read her mind—and the possibility completely unnerved her.

For too long he sat there, simply staring, his slight smile highlighting the dimple on his left cheek. She tried to not squirm as she waited for him to answer, but darned if she was going to ask the question again. He'd heard her, and she could wait it out as well as he could.

After another agonizing minute Ken slipped his hand away from her, the caress giving her shivers, then he moved closer and lightly traced the tip of his forefinger down her cheek, barely making contact. "What do you think?"

"I think you're playing games." He'd thrown her off balance, taken the upper hand, and now she grappled for some control, trying to convince herself that he hadn't rattled her completely. "Games two can play as well as one." With a deft movement, she caught his hand and pressed it against her face. His skin was still rough, masculine, just as she remembered it, and the sensation of skin against skin set her head to spinning.

Trying for a sultry smile, she moved her head ever so slightly until her lips grazed the side of his hand.

She pressed a light kiss there, wondering if the touch was stirring in him the same memories that were dancing through her head. "You didn't answer my question. Are we talking about sex?"

She'd pitched her voice low and was rewarded to see him swallow.

"Not just sex. Decadence. A wild time the likes of which we never got to have before."

Because you left. The unspoken words rang in her head, both an invitation and an accusation.

"Do you think I owe you?" Her mind was all twisted up.

Again, she wasn't sure if she should be angry he was using her, or flattered he still cared. Her sensible side said she should be angry, but the rest of her— the part that had never completely got him out of her mind—was intrigued. He was the man she'd wanted more than anything—except, of course, for her career.

Still, to use sex as the bargaining chip between them… She gnawed on her lip, unsure what to do or how to react. Unsure, for that matter, if she really believed her ears.

Five years ago Ken had been such an innocent. The media may have pegged him—rightly—as a go-getter, but newspapers had a way of focusing on the sensational. No interview or article had ever shown a hint of the sweet, small-town boy Lisa had loved. His Texas charm had meshed with his business savvy, and the combination was potent. It had certainly knocked Lisa off her feet.

But he'd always been the one to back off from

moving too fast. She might have been the wild, small-town girl turned loose in the big city. But Ken had never lost himself the way she had. He'd always been focused, sure of what he wanted, and confident he could get it. But he was never untoward, and he never played dirty.

So for him to be suggesting a night of sin and sex…well, the whole thing was a little unnerving. Of course—since she was being honest—she had to admit it was also extremely titillating. Small-town Ken playing sex games. Had he really changed that much? Or was the scent of real desire in the air?

She didn't know. Maybe Ken truly wanted her—wanted to have a taste of what they'd lost when she'd left. More likely, he just wanted revenge—the opportunity to show her what she'd missed out on, to tease and to torture her with sex and seduction. Lord knew, he'd had his share of women, at least according to the papers. In the eyes of the media, Ken Harper was an accomplished lover.

"Lisa?"

She gnawed lightly on her lower lip. What other choice did she have? Without Ken, her plans would completely fall apart. He was her best chance, her last chance. And maybe she owed him. After all, she was the one who left him.

His slow grin held all sorts of erotic promises, and she closed her eyes to block a tremble. Who was she kidding? She wasn't agreeing because she *owed* him. She was agreeing because she wanted him—had wanted him for years.

But she had her price, too, and she sat up straighter, trying to focus on the fact that she was in Los Angeles for work, not to sleep with Ken Harper. "Yes," she said, with one curt nod of her head. "But on one condition."

He quirked a brow and leaned back, the epitome of the cool negotiator. "And what condition might that be?"

She flashed what she hoped was a saucy grin. "More help, of course."

To her relief, he laughed. "Okay. I'll bite. With what?"

"The other locations." She glanced down at the tabletop, then back up at him through her eyelashes. "If you're the Casanova the media makes you out to be, surely you can help me find a few sexy locations."

He didn't admit or deny, and she realized she was disappointed. She'd wanted him to say he wasn't a Casanova, that the media had done a typical hype job, and he was still the same old Ken. But he was silent, just sitting there with his chin propped on his clasped hands as he watched her.

Finally he nodded. "It's a deal."

"It is?"

"Absolutely."

"Oh."

An amused smile danced on his lips. "Disappointed? You didn't think I'd say no, did you?"

"No...I..." Flustered, she decided it was better to just stay quiet. The truth was, she wasn't disappointed at all. Quite the opposite, and the feeling unsettled her.

"In fact," he continued, leaning closer, "I think this may work out just fine. Who knows? Maybe we can even explore my side of the bargain while we're checking out those locations."

She couldn't answer, could only nod and wonder what she'd gotten herself into.

Because the truth was, though she wouldn't admit it to Ken, not in a million years, she'd been thinking that exact same thing.

"Homework?" Tim asked from the doorway.

Startled, Ken looked up from tourist map of Los Angeles he'd been studying. "Sort of. I'm taking Lisa out tonight, and I'm trying to decide where to go."

"A real date?" Tim's voice rose with interest. "I guess I was wrong. I thought you had some decadent little plan worked out."

"No comment," Ken said. His plan was in place, all right—a plan forged in the fire of revenge. And now he wasn't sure that putting it into motion was one of the brighter things he'd ever done. He'd spent less than two hours with her that morning, and he could still smell her scent on his clothes, could close his eyes and picture every line on her face.

"Well, now I'm curious." Tim folded himself into the chair opposite Ken's desk, his long legs out to the side. "Spill it. What are you up to?"

Ken hesitated only a second, but Tim was his best friend. He'd never kept a secret from him, and he didn't intend to start now. "I told you she was here scouting locations, right?" At Tim's nod, he filled in the rest of the story. "So I said I'd help her find some locations."

Tim's brow lifted. "In exchange for finding her in your bed?"

"Something like that."

His friend shook his head slowly. "You're in over your head."

"I don't think so," Ken said, even though he'd thought exactly that only moments before.

"No?"

"I've got it under control."

"Then why *are* you doing this?"

Ken stood, not sure he wanted to examine his motives, afraid of what he'd find in his heart if he looked too closely. A mishmash of emotions washed through him as he stalked to the window. Looking down at the street below, he tried to sort out his feelings, but they were too wild, too raw. Finally he turned back to Tim. "It's something I need to do."

"I never pegged you as the revenge type."

Nor had he. But Lisa got under his skin. When he thought about her, his blood boiled, the pressure building until he craved release. He needed something from her, he just wasn't sure what. Revenge? Or something else?

Tim was looking at him, a curious expression on his face.

"What?" Ken demanded, trying to relax.

"I'm just wondering if it is revenge."

"What do you mean?"

"The lady's special. You've always thought so. And now you have the chance to show her what she missed out on. So maybe you're not doing it to torment her. Maybe you're doing it with the hope that she'll stay."

"That's ridiculous," he said automatically.

"Is it? Remember who you're talking to, buddy. I'm the one who roomed with you while my condo was being renovated. Maybe you can pull a fast one on someone else, but I'm the one who knows you still keep her engagement ring in a box on your chest of drawers."

Ken's heart twisted as he wondered if Tim was right, even as he desperately hoped he was wrong. When he faced him, he knew his expression was clear, emotionless. "I don't have any illusions. I'm fine."

But he wasn't so sure. The fact was, Lisa had managed to edge her way into his life again. He had a sneaking suspicion that his original intention of making her weak with lust was going to backfire. And at the end of the day, he'd be the one with his heart hanging out to dry once again.

Mentally, he shook his head. He had a plan, and he was going to see it through. He was going to show her what she'd missed out on. He was going to make her pay in all sorts of decadent and erotic ways. And he was going to get her out of his system once and for all. *Finito*. Kaput. End of story.

Determined, he slipped behind his desk, then

leaned back in the chair. "Do you want to sit there psychoanalyzing me all night, or do you want to help me?"

For a second he thought Tim was going to leave, but then he shifted in the chair, settling in more comfortably. "I'm game. What do you need?"

"Locations. I'm supposed to help her find places to film. How the hell do I know what's sexy in L.A.?"

"Ken, my man, you've come to the right place."

Ken stifled a chuckle. "Glad to hear it. But what makes you such a connoisseur?"

"Chic magazines."

Ken made a swooshing motion over his head. "Come again?"

"When Melinda left, she didn't forward her subscriptions. I've been getting all these damn magazines for months."

"Okay." He held his hands out in confusion. "And…"

Tim half shrugged, looking slightly sheepish. "So I figured I'd read them. Maybe get some insight into the female psyche. Figured if I did, maybe the next girl would hang around longer."

Ken bit the inside of his cheek to keep from laughing as he pictured Tim—six-foot-three and two hundred and twenty pounds—sacked out on the sofa reading *Cosmopolitan*. "Is it working?"

"Nah. You just can't figure women out, with or without a guidebook. But these magazines do have some interesting articles. One of them's been doing an article every month about fabulous places to do the wild thing in various big cities.''

"Los Angeles?"

"Last month's issue."

"Must be karma."

"I'm not so sure," Tim said. "If this thing back-fires, I sure as hell don't want it on my conscience that I gave you the roadmap for seduction.''

LISA KNEW she should be working, but somehow she couldn't concentrate. Ever since breakfast she'd been on edge, wondering what Ken had in store for her that evening. After Hugo's, she'd driven around the city. She told herself she was looking for exotic, erotic locations, but somehow she ended up on Melrose Avenue in front of the trendy boutiques that lined the famous street.

She didn't need a new outfit; she couldn't afford a new outfit. Yet somehow her credit card seemed to take control and steer her into a brightly lit shop with a flirty red dress in the window.

A bell above the door jingled as she stepped inside, and a salesgirl with magenta hair and a stud through her nose bopped over, gum smacking. "Can I help you?"

"Oh, uh, no. I'm just looking." Lisa glanced around. Everything in the store was just as cute as the red dress. Considering she was broke, this was going to be torture.

"Take your time. There's more in the back." She pointed vaguely toward the rear of the store, then flounced back to the cash register to ring up a sequined purple tank top held by a woman in a tailored business suit.

Each rack seemed to hold a minimum of one truly bizarre outfit, balanced by another outfit so cute and perfect that Lisa mourned having been out of steady work for so long. She had her eye on a green silk shorts set with a matching jacket and tank top, when the salesgirl came back over.

"That's a great outfit. You can, like, wear it to work, but it's also great for dates for the weekend or whatever."

"It's great," Lisa agreed.

"Want me to take it to the dressing room for you?"

"No, thanks," Lisa said, fully intending to announce that she was just browsing. Instead, though, her traitorous mouth took over and said, "I'm looking for something for a date."

"Ohhhhh!" The girl nodded. "Something fun and flirty. Gotcha."

Lisa mumbled something noncommittal, totally irritated with herself. This wasn't a *date* date. She was not *dating* Ken. She was going out with him, yes, but only because that was his condition for helping her, not because there was anything left between them. It was about the job. *Job, job, job.*

"You okay?"

Lisa nodded. "Fine. The thing is, it's not exactly a date. It's a business deal, too."

"Colleague or opponent?"

She frowned. "Pardon?"

The girl ran a hand through her hair, spiking it and making Lisa wonder if magenta sparks were going to start flying. "Is the guy someone you work with, or someone you're trying to get something from?"

"Oh. The second."

The girl grinned, and Lisa saw a smear of purple lipstick on her front tooth. "I know just the dress." She bounced toward the window and took down the red dress, the one Lisa'd been eyeing. The one Lisa knew better than to wear on a date with Ken.

"Oh, I don't think so..."

"Trust me. This dress will seal any deal."

Lisa licked her lips. True, she wanted Ken's help, but what she didn't want was to seem too eager to participate in his rather decadent conditions—no matter how titillating the idea might be. If she were smart, she'd wear her denim skirt and a sweater, comfortable and casual.

Except her brain didn't seem to be calling the shots, and she found herself nodding and reaching for the dress. "I guess it wouldn't hurt just to try it on."

Probably smelling a sale, the girl pretty much danced toward the dressing room, picking up accessories as she went. Lisa followed meekly, feeling a bit like a child following the pied piper. By the time they hit the dressing room, the girl had gathered the red dress, a sequined bolero-length sweater jacket, strappy red sandals, and a red leather clutch bag.

"It's all yours. Let me know if the size isn't right."

Nodding, Lisa took a deep breath and entered no-man's land. Once she went in, she knew she wasn't leaving without that dress. And once she got it on, she was even more sure. It was, in a word, stunning. The material was a rayon-silk blend that felt fabulous against her skin. And skin was pretty much all that was against it, at least up top, because the upper portion of the dress was two simple crisscrosses of gathered material sewn together at the neck.

The design accentuated her cleavage, leaving a bare back and very little to the imagination. The rest of the dress was just as provocative. A tight waist flared out into a dancer's skirt that could, if she wanted, reveal all with a simple twirl.

The salesgirl had done a good job guessing Lisa's shoe size, too, and the sandals fit like a dream. Taking a deep breath, she pushed the dressing room curtain aside and stepped out, wanting to take a look at the ensemble in the three-way mirror.

"Ouch! Girl, that dress is hot!"

Lisa did a little mini twirl in front of the mirror, careful to not let the skirt flare too high, and had to agree. "It is, isn't it?"

"Is he cute?"

An image of Ken's piercing blue eyes and solid jaw flashed in her mind. "Better than cute. He's handsome."

The girl, who never seemed to stay completely still, bobbed a bit more and clapped her hands. "Awesome. You've got to get it. You look like a movie star."

Lisa glanced over her shoulder, catching her reflection in the three-way mirror. It truly was one heck of a dress. She felt sexy. Confident. As if she could take over the world, and certainly as though she could seal one little deal.

Besides, the truth was, she wanted to see his eyes when he saw her in this outfit.

Knowing her credit card would come close to keeling over from the strain, she nodded. "I'll take it."

"Excellent. Shoes and purse, too?"

"What the hell? It's only plastic."

The girl grinned. "Does that mean you want the sweater, too?" She reached into the dressing room and emerged with the dainty thing. "It gets cold near the beach at night…"

She let the words hang until Lisa rolled her eyes and waved her hand. "Fine. Add it in. I can't do much more damage."

"Trust me," the girl said a few minutes later at the cash register. "I totally wouldn't steer you wrong. This is one hot outfit. It's going to, like, totally, clinch your deal."

Lisa took the shopping bag and nodded. The girl was undoubtedly right. But what deal would get clinched? Her deal for Ken's location? Or Ken's deal…for her?

6

KEN'S PRIVATE OFFICES were located on the mezzanine level of the Bellisimo, adjacent to the restaurant. He'd spent the hours since the lunch rush pouring over Tim's magazine, thinking and rethinking locations for Lisa's movie—locations for a seduction.

Tonight he was going to start out sweet and simple, crafting an erotic buildup for maximum effect. From the way he'd come on at breakfast, she undoubtedly expected him to urge her into his bed for a long night of sensuous delights. As tempting as that sounded, Ken intended to throw her off balance. He'd start out romantic and work his way up to seductive. By the time Lisa ended up in his bed, Ken wanted her desperate for him. His plan might have been formed in anger, but that didn't change the bottom line. He intended to have a good time—a damn good time—when Lisa ended up in his bed.

They'd agreed to meet in front of the restaurant at seven, so at five he wrapped up, putting away Tim's magazine and the tourist map of L.A. The hotel was hosting a pharmaceutical convention, and he stepped from his office into a crowd of people leaving the two smaller ballrooms.

He moved with the group toward the elevators and stood pressed between a tall woman in a tailored suit and a short man in a sweater vest as he waited for the elevator to arrive. When it did, the crowd practically pushed him on, and he moved to the back, only noticing when he turned around that Lisa was in the front near the control panel.

"Twenty, please," he said.

Her hand raised to punch the button, and he could tell the exact moment she recognized his voice. Her shoulders stiffened, and she cocked her head then turned around to face him.

"Hi," he said.

Her cheeks flushed, and he wondered what she was thinking. "Hi."

She shifted and he noticed the garment bag she was holding. "Shopping?" The dress was blood-red, with not too much material on top, and he couldn't help but imagine how absolutely gorgeous she'd look in it. He imagined her pressed against him, his hand cupping her bare back. Feeling himself harden, he shook his head, trying to rein in his newfound lust. "For our date, I hope."

Her cheeks flushed, and her eyes darted to the other passengers as she pushed the bag behind her. "No." She lifted her chin, her voice indignant, and Ken remembered how adorable she looked when cornered.

That he could still rattle her thrilled him in some deep, masculine way. She'd wounded his pride, and it was reassuring to know it had cost her at least something when she'd left him.

"I, uh, just needed a few things," Lisa said.

"Including a super-sexy little red dress?" Because he couldn't help it, he let his gaze roam over her body, his blood pulsing hot as he imagined those sweet curves under his fingertips, when he met her eyes he saw annoyance and something else. Something potent.

Before he could analyze her look, she blinked and straightened, leaving only a put-out expression. "So why are you going up to the rooms?"

He stifled a grin, amused by her efforts to change the subject. "Just heading home."

The elevator stopped and the conventioneers stepped out. He moved toward her, taking advantage of the space they left. A thin veneer of hurt and anger surrounded him every time he got near to her. But despite that—or perhaps because of it—the need to touch her almost overwhelmed him. He fisted his hands at his sides. He wasn't going to. It was becoming a matter of principle; he was going to build up his touches until they were both insane with need. Of course, he was close to that point already, a fact that left him a little concerned about the wisdom of his plan. But he didn't intend to back down now.

"Home?"

"Something wrong with that?"

Her forehead creased, and he moved nearer, the floral scent of her perfume driving him a little insane. "You live here? In the hotel?"

"Moved in a few years ago." He didn't mention he'd moved in after she'd left town.

He propped his hand on the wall behind her as he leaned closer. "Besides, I've got everything I need here. A little kitchen, a living room…" He ducked his head until his lips grazed her hair, hoping he was driving her as crazy as he was driving himself. Summoning every ounce of willpower in his body, he resisted the urge to taste her earlobe. "A bedroom."

"Oh." She stepped backward until she was pressed against the wall, but couldn't escape the circle of his arm. "I, um, why?"

He shrugged, not comfortable examining his reasons. "Seemed easier than mowing the lawn. Keeps me closer to work." He spoke with a light tone, but she squinted, as if she knew she wasn't hearing the full story.

The elevator stopped on fifteen, and Ken was grateful for the reprieve. A woman wearing a terry-cloth robe over a bathing suit stepped on. "Could you hit the pool level, please?"

Since they had company, Ken stepped back, releasing Lisa from the circle of his arms. She rushed to push the elevator button, clearly relieved to have reclaimed some personal space. Lord, he wanted to touch her. Wanted to reach out and pull her close and demand answers. Wanted to possess her, body and mind, until the hurt melted and the fury faded and he had his heart back.

Stepping further back, he curled his hands into fists, concentrating all his energy on keeping control. Tim was right. He was playing with fire, and he was the one that was going to get burned.

The elevator stopped on eighteen, and the woman for the pool got off. Alone, they stood there, not looking at each other, the air practically crackling between them, until they reached the twenty-fourth floor and the elevator doors slid open again.

"I—I'm sorry," she said. "I guess I forgot to hit your floor."

"No problem. I can find my way home."

She draped the bag over her arm and straightened the strap on her purse. "Well, this is my stop."

As she passed by him, he caught her arm. "Lisa."

She turned, eyes wide and curious. "Yes?"

"Wear the dress."

Her lips twitched, and her gaze drifted over him, her examination so slow and thorough he hardened under the caress of her gaze. After a moment she blinked, then moved into the hallway, glancing at him over her shoulder. "Maybe I will," she said with a shrug. "For you, maybe I will."

"DO YOU HAVE AN UPDATE for me?" Even from across the country, Winston's voice sounded crisp, clear and no-nonsense.

"I've only been here a day and a half." She'd been debating wearing the dress when he called, and now she pulled the bedspread off and wrapped it around her naked shoulders, not wanting to talk to Winston in her underwear.

"A lot can happen in a day. I locked in two locations in San Francisco this morning. Nice town, San Francisco. If you don't come through for me, looks like I'll be spending some time there—and finding someone else to be my producer."

Her stomach lurched. She couldn't let him pick San Francisco. She needed this too badly. She hesitated only briefly, then took a deep breath and took the plunge. "The truth is, I made a deal with Harper."

"It's all set? You got the restaurant?"

She crossed her fingers. "I'm meeting him in an hour to go over the details." Not exactly a lie.

"And the rest of the locations?"

"Ken's going with me to scout a few later tonight."

He grunted. "Well, I've got to give Greg credit. Looks like you were the best man for the job."

After he said goodbye, she took ten deep breaths, wondering if the fates were going to punish her for spinning little white lies. Not that she'd said anything truly inaccurate. But she hadn't exactly left Winston with the full picture. Hadn't mentioned, for example, that the deal still needed to be sealed—with herself.

She shook her head, determined to be Scarlett O'Hara and deal with that tomorrow. Right now she had enough to deal with—such as figuring out what exactly Ken wanted. And deciding what the heck she was going to wear while he took it.

She dropped the bedspread and headed back toward the mirror. She'd already put the dress on and taken it off five times, and now she really needed to make up her mind and get her makeup on or she was going to be late.

Making a face, she ran her hands through her hair,

feeling frazzled and anything but in control. She couldn't blow this. *She couldn't.* Hell, Winston thought the deal was locked in. He was probably already packing his bags and making reservations at his favorite Los Angeles hotel.

She gave her reflection a long, steady look. "But it's not a done deal until you meet his conditions."

Thinking about what that meant, she ran her hands over her breasts and her stomach, closing her eyes as she imagined Ken touching her. He wanted to, that much she knew. She'd seen it in his eyes at breakfast and again in the elevator. He wanted to touch her, wanted to make love to her. But she'd also seen anger buried beneath those icy-blue eyes.

Ken might want her—but he also wanted her to pay.

Wondering exactly what the price would be, she licked her lips as she ran the material of the dress between her fingers. Silky and seductive, the dress made her feel feminine and powerful. After only a moment's hesitation, she slipped it on, the material as soft as a lover's touch. She twirled in front of the mirror, realizing she wasn't a whole lot more dressed wearing it than not wearing it.

She knew he was angry—that was more than clear. But there'd also been a hunger in his eyes when she'd gotten off the elevator at her floor, as though he was imagining her in the dress—and out of it. Truth be told, she liked knowing that hunger was for her. She hadn't felt feminine in a long, long time. And despite the bizarre circumstances, the feeling was intoxicating.

Closing her eyes, she sat on the edge of the bed, her body thrumming from the memory of the way his face had looked before the elevator doors had slid closed. The slight curve of his lips, the dark passion in his eyes.

With a sigh, she grazed her hands lightly over the material, feeling it caress her thighs, her skin warming despite the coolness of the fabric. Her nipples tightened, and she stroked her hands upward, cupping her breasts as she teased her nipples with her thumbs, all the while imagining Ken's mouth, warm and wet, laving her breasts.

Moaning, she lay back on the bed, knowing she should stop, but not wanting to. Her body burned, her breath coming rough and jagged. Ever since she'd seen him, she'd been tense, her libido out of control, and now she wanted the release, needed it, even. Needed to get it out of her system before she saw him again and did something she'd regret.

There wasn't much to the top of the dress, and she slipped her hand under the material. Her nipple was tight and tingly, and she stroked it lightly with the palm of her hand, her touch little more than a tease. She imagined Ken's hands on her, and the sensations rippled through her, the warmth filling her belly and pooling between her thighs. His imaginary kisses trailed down her body, teasing her thighs, urging her legs apart.

She trembled, entirely lost in the moment except

for the tiny part of her that wished she weren't thinking of him.

Dipping her fingers down, she touched herself, her
fingers stroking the material of the dress along the
apex of her thighs. She sighed, the sound low in her
throat. Arching her back, she grazed the tips of her
fingers up her thigh, sliding the material up her leg,
needing to feel the cool rush of air as the material
drifted over her. Her fingers traced the edge of her
panties, then trailed over the damp silk at the crotch.

She imagined Ken leaning over her, his lips near
hers, his rough hands stroking her sides, his body hard
against hers. The air did nothing to cool her burning
body, and she rubbed her fingers in a circle over the
damp material, her breath coming faster and faster
until she came with a gasp, her body warm and trembling as she curled up into a little ball, trying to keep
a hold on some tiny bit of the ecstacy.

As she was hugging her knees to her chest, sanity
returned, and she wondered what the hell she'd just
done. And why. She felt better, yet somehow she felt
worse—not to mention scared. In just a little bit she'd
see him again. Had she gotten him out of her system?
Or had she only primed the pump?

"You're a mess," she whispered.

It was true. And she knew one other thing for certain—no way was she going out with Ken Harper
wearing that damn red dress.

"SO WHERE ARE WE GOING?" Lisa asked.

They were in his Jaguar, the top down, and he

turned to get a better look at her. She hadn't worn the dress, and he'd felt a twinge of disappointment when he'd seen her standing in the lobby wearing a knee-length denim skirt and a simple T-shirt. She still looked sexy as hell, but he'd been hoping that she'd wear the dress because she knew he wanted it.

She's not doing this to make you happy, Harper. She's doing it to get what she wants. Business. Only business.

And wasn't that always the way? An invisible band tightened around his chest as the inevitable, infuriating truth set in—Lisa was there because she needed something. Just as she'd left five years ago because he *couldn't* help. Now she was back because he could.

Dammit.

He resisted the urge to pound his palm against the steering wheel, instead gripping the wheel so hard he was probably going to leave permanent indentions.

She was there for business, and he was there to exorcise the past. Not romance. Not love. Not even a date. He needed to remember that. Needed to keep it foremost in his mind before he lost himself again.

"Ken?" She was twisting her hands in her lap. "Did you hear me? Where are we going?"

"Don't you trust me?"

"Don't you have to work tonight?" A nonanswer.

"Nope. I'm all yours." He *should* be working. Not only were Sundays usually busy, but he and Tim made a habit of going over the specials for the next week every Sunday night.

He flashed her a relaxed grin, then reached out and closed his palm over her clasped hands. "Besides, I *am* working." He gave her hand a gentle squeeze, delighting in the softness of her skin. "We're scouting locations, remember?"

"Right." She shivered slightly. *Good.*

"Cold?" he asked, certain her shiver had nothing to do with the temperature.

"A little. The ocean air."

They were cruising south on the Pacific Coast Highway toward Santa Monica. Beside her, the sun had begun its nightly descent into the ocean, and a wash of orange and purple filled the sky, reflecting off the gold of her hair. It was a beautiful, magical tableau, and he wanted to hold the moment close to his heart.

But it was all an illusion. They weren't lovers out for a twilight drive. Instead she was sitting next to him, her mind probably going a million miles a minute as she wondered where he was taking her...and what was in store for her once they got there. He wondered how long she could hold out before she asked again.

"Ken..."

Fifteen seconds. He stifled a grin as he turned to her. Her hair was blowing free, and he tucked a strand behind her ear, the tiny moment of intimacy tightening the band around his heart even more. "You'll see when we get there."

"Hmm." She turned in the seat to face him better,

then tied her hair back with a rubber band she'd dug from her purse. "Will you tell me if I guess?"

He answered the tease in her voice with a slow smile. "You want me to tell you if you're cold, warm...or hot?"

"Yes, well, um..." She shifted in her seat again, frowning at the countryside. "Are we stopping in Santa Monica or going farther south?"

"Where would you like to go?"

"You're the one calling the shots."

He took his eyes off the road long enough to look at her. "Am I? I wasn't completely sure."

"Trust me," she said, meeting his eyes. "I'm completely at your disposal."

"How nice for me." He'd pitched his voice low and was rewarded by the spot of color that touched her cheeks.

She cleared her throat and sat up straighter. "Do you plan to let me in on what you've got in store for me? Or is that as much of a secret as where we're going?"

"I thought you liked surprises."

"I thought I did, too. But this one's got me a little on edge."

In that case, he'd already accomplished at least part of his mission. "It's just dinner, Lisa. And I'm not the Marquis de Sade. Just relax and enjoy the drive."

ENJOY THE DRIVE. Lisa leaned back in her seat, wondering how he expected her to do that without knowing what he had planned. She was completely at his mercy and flying blind.

And considering her little episode in the hotel room earlier, she was also more than a little...well, on edge. She wanted to keep as much control as possible, and he wasn't helping by keeping her in the dark.

Scowling, she cast him a sideways glance. "Not even a hint?"

He reached over and flipped on the radio, fiddling with the dial until he found an oldies station. He didn't say a word, just started humming along with a Beatles's song.

Frustrated, she crossed her arms over her chest and scowled. Ken could be stubborn when he wanted to be, and she knew better than to try to drag out information that he didn't want to reveal. Still, she wished he'd say something, anything. She'd agreed to his absurd condition, and that meant that tonight she was his. Part of her couldn't believe she'd agreed to such a trade, and another part of her—the bigger part, if she wanted to be honest—couldn't wait to get started with the bargain.

The road curved, and they had to part company with the beach. She watched, trying to pay attention to where they were, as he maneuvered the streets of Santa Monica. Adorable stucco bungalows lined shaded streets, set back just far enough from the main roads for a little peace and quiet.

Lisa took a deep breath. Even several streets inland she could taste the salt of the ocean in the air, and once again she was struck by how much she'd missed

Los Angeles. She'd always assumed she'd live in one of those little bungalows, fighting traffic every morning to get to the studio before the phone started ringing.

Years ago she'd thought Ken wanted the same thing. At the time he'd been renting a three-bedroom house just off Wilshire with an orange tree in the backyard. He'd loved the house, even though he never had time to spend in it. And it was for that reason that his news that he'd moved into the hotel had not only surprised her, but concerned her.

She wondered if he'd given up his plans to open a diner, too. She almost asked, but she was pretty sure he had. Surely another Ken Harper restaurant would have made the news. But she'd never heard about a diner.

"You okay?"

Real concern reflected in his eyes, and she nodded, deciding not to ask about the diner. Their arrangement might be sexual, but that didn't mean it was personal. Not anymore. It had quit being personal the night she'd caught the red-eye to New York five years ago.

"I'm fine." She conjured a smile. "It's just...just that I always loved this neighborhood."

He rested his palm against the back of her neck and rubbed lightly. "I remember."

"Oh." She frowned, flustered. "Right. Of course." She turned to squint at him as a new thought occurred to her. "Is this coincidence, or are you trying to throw me off balance?"

His fingers stroked upward, soothing her tense muscles. "What do you think?"

She couldn't look at him. "I'm not sure what to think anymore."

"Then don't think. Just enjoy."

"I'm not supposed to enjoy. I'm supposed to be working." And she was so on edge, not knowing what to expect, that enjoyment didn't seem within the realm of possibility.

"Just relax," he said, reading her mind, as usual.

"How do you do that?"

"Do what?"

"Know what I'm thinking."

His magic fingers grazed the back of her neck, warm and tempting. Her nipples peaked, straining against the thin lace of her bra, and she silently cursed, telling herself it was the cool evening air and not the result of Ken's touch.

"I know you, Lisa." He took his hand away to shift gears, and she felt herself relax, even as a blanket of disappointment surrounded her. "I've always known you."

"Do you? Because I don't think I know you." The Ken she remembered was solid and dependable. Sexy, yes, but not seductive. Had Ken changed? Had she? Or was she reacting not to him, but to the situation?

"Did you ever know me?" he asked.

She swallowed. "Of course." But she couldn't meet his eyes. Instead she looked out the window so that he couldn't see her expression. Had she focused so much on her work that she never really got to know him?

"Mmm."

At his noncommital response, she turned to look at him, but didn't try to reassure him.

"Well," he said, "it doesn't matter now, does it?" With the side of his hand, he stroked her cheek. "That was all a long time ago, right?"

Her breath caught, but she managed a nod. "A lifetime."

He glided to a stop in front of a valet stand. "Hungry?"

"Supporting the competition?"

He flashed a grin as he handed the keys to the valet. "They make a fabulous crème brûlée."

"Tim'll have your head if he hears you."

"You'll keep my guilty secret, though, won't you?" He slipped his arm around her waist, and she leaned against him automatically. His arm tightened just slightly, and she realized with a start her proximity to him. For a split second she considered jumping away, but she hadn't been held in a long, long time and it felt rather nice. Nice, but disconcerting.

When he'd said he wanted her as a condition of helping her, she'd assumed he'd meant sex—wild, hot, passionate sex. But this was Ken she was dealing with. Sweet, innocent, Southern Ken. She should have realized he wasn't the seduction-for-revenge type. Flirting, sure. But wild sex? Not his style.

Not at all.

And damn if she wasn't disappointed.

7

ALICIA DRUMMED her fingers on the vanity, her eyes trained on the phone she'd just hung up. She'd known Tina Strombard ever since the little twit had interned for her while Alicia had anchored the news. Now that Tina was Winston Miller's receptionist, Alicia'd resorted to sending the twit presents. So far, the payoff hadn't been particularly amazing—a few tidbits about casting, early news about where Miller was filming his latest, general crap Alicia could chat about during her morning show.

But today...well, today she'd hit pay dirt. And she was pissed as hell.

Not one day had passed since Ken Harper had practically patted her on the head and shoved her out the door. He'd made it clear. No filming in his precious restaurant. Certainly can't do a favor for a woman he used to date. Nothing that might upset the oh-so-mysterious mystique of his precious restaurant. And now he'd gone and opened the door to a full production crew. Not only would they likely be filming for weeks, but Oxygen was going to end up splashed all over a movie screen.

Bastard.

Her fingernails clicked on the wood as her fury

grew. What was it Tina had said? Something about sending some tramp location scout to convince Harper to open the restaurant. Well, she must have been awfully persuasive.

She wondered just how persuavive. Had the little bitch just spread her legs and invited Harper in? Alicia imagined so, and that really burned. She'd offered Ken the same, and he'd practically turned up his nose.

What the hell did the little tramp have that she didn't have? *Nothing.* Alicia had her own talk show, for God's sake. And there was no way in hell Alicia was going to believe that Ken preferred a tramp to someone of Alicia's caliber. No way at all.

And she certainly couldn't believe that his bimbo location scout was so amazing in bed that Ken would do a complete one-eighty. No, that just wasn't possible. Something else was going on.

The little witch had something on Ken. Some bit of dirt. Some piece of gossip. Something.

But what?

She didn't have a clue. But she hadn't earned an Emmy because she didn't have instincts. She had excellent instincts.

Something wasn't right. The kind of something that Gavin wanted as spice for her show.

Alicia intended to figure out exactly what that something was.

"SO DID I LIE?" Ken asked.

Lisa looked up, surprise in her beautiful eyes. "Lie?"

They were walking along his favorite section of the Third Street Promenade, near the topiaries designed to look like giant dinosaurs. He stopped at a cart selling espresso and ordered two cappuccinos. "About the crème brûlée. It was the best ever, right?"

She laughed. "It was pretty good," she said.

"I've got to figure out a way to get their pastry chef to come work for me." He paid the vendor and took the drinks.

"Well, just be your usual charming self and I'm sure the chef will fall all over himself to do anything for you."

"You think?"

They stopped at the corner, and she turned just long enough to flash him a saucy look. "Absolutely. Isn't that how you got where you are today? Your famous charm?" She cleared her throat, then ran her tongue over her lips before looking away. "Isn't that why I'm here?"

Sadly, it wasn't. She was there because she needed him. Nothing more, nothing less.

Except...

There had been moments that had seemed almost normal. Moments when he felt almost right, almost whole. They'd had a wonderful dinner. No games, no double entendres. Just a man and a woman sharing a meal and conversation. They'd talked about everything and nothing—certainly nothing important. She hadn't mentioned her movie; he hadn't mentioned their deal. It had almost been like old times.

And now he realized that she was about to burst with curiosity. On his mental scoreboard, he chalked one up for the home team. Before he was through, he intended to score a touchdown.

He slipped his arm around her waist as they turned toward the beach. "You're not here because I'm just so damn charming. You're here because you need me, and I insisted you be here."

"True." She tilted her head to look him straight in the eye, not the least bit intimidated by the censure in his voice. "But you have to agree you're pretty persuasive."

"Persuasive." He mulled over the word, amused by how she was holding her own. "And here I was hoping for handsome and sexy. At least as hot as...who is it all the women like so much? Mel Gibson? Or is it Russell Crowe now?" He stroked his fingers over the sleeve of her T-shirt, moving down until his fingertips caressed her bare skin. "Either way, I'm willing to settle for persuasive."

"Oh." Her hard-fought cool was slipping.

He put his arm around her shoulder to pull her close. "Sure you're not cold?"

"No." She glanced down at his fingers grazing the goose bumps on her skin. "Um, I mean, yes. Yes. It's chilly."

He took his hand from her shoulder long enough to slide out of his jacket and put it around her shoulders.

"Thanks."

"You're welcome."

They strolled another block in silence, and Ken fought the urge to touch her again. When they reached the next street, he gave in and took her hand, part of him irritated with himself for giving in to desire so easily, another part of him feeling a little like a high school kid out on his first date. Ironic, since the plans he had for Lisa were anything but prom-night innocent.

As they walked, she looked down at their clasped hands and then back up at him, a smile and a question in her brown eyes. "How about now?"

"Now what?"

"Will you tell me where we're going now?"

"Wouldn't you rather it be a surprise?"

"I've had a lot of surprises already, and I think there's a lot more to come. I think I'd like to know this one little thing."

"For you, anything." He let go of her hand and spread his arm out in front of him. "We're here."

She blinked and looked across the street, then back into his face. He kept his expression serious.

"Here?" she repeated. "The Santa Monica Pier?"

"Absolutely." He extended his arm in invitation. "Shall we?"

She shook her head, half smiling, but she linked her arm through his, and they walked across the street to the boardwalk leading up to the pier. They walked in silence past the vendors selling cotton candy and roses. To their right, waves broke on the beach that stretched out below the pier, the froth lit up in the moonlight. To the left, a Ferris wheel turned, giving tourists and natives a romantic view of the city skyline.

"Remember when we came here?" she asked.

Of course he did. "Every detail." He'd never forgotten a second of their first date.

"Oh, look!" She turned, tugging him with her as she rushed to the glassed-in building on their left. "Well, damn. The carousel's not running tonight." She tossed him a sad smile. "Too bad."

"Would you have taken a ride with me if it were?"

"Why not?"

"We rode it on our first date." He heard the harshness in his voice and cursed himself for not keeping a better check on his emotions. "I guess I'm not sure if riding it tonight would be nostalgic or callous."

"Listen, Ken, I don't know what you think…" When she turned to face him, he saw a tear in her eye, and felt a moment of guilt, wondering if he'd put it there. She straightened her shoulders, the gesture giving her some semblance of control. "Well, I have some idea, considering this little deal you put together, but I want you to know you're not exactly right." Her voice was firm.

"How do you know I'm not right if you don't know what I think?"

"I'm relatively intelligent," she said. "And I just want you to know I never meant to hurt you."

He opened his mouth to tell her she'd done a damn good job of it anyway, but he caught himself before the words were out. He wasn't there to fight about the past; he was there to move on.

She licked her lips. "I'm sorry I never told you that before, but when I left I was thinking of my job. I thought..." She trailed off. "Never mind."

With effort, he swallowed, managing to force down the lump of tenseness in his throat. He didn't want to hear her excuses and apologies, and he feared he was going to give in. He was *that* close to pulling her into his arms and telling her that all was forgiven. But it *wasn't* forgiven or forgotten. And he'd do well to not harp on some sentimental image of how it used to be.

"You thought what?" he asked, knowing he shouldn't be opening that door.

She tilted her head back to look at him, her lashes damp with unshed tears. "I thought we could still see each other."

He bit back a mirthless laugh. "Even though you'd just run off to New York with another man? Oh, sure. I can see how you thought that had all the makings of a fine relationship."

"It was a great opportunity. And I wasn't dating him. Not then. He was just my boss."

Ken bristled, not sure he believed that. "Even if, you were still thousands of miles away."

"Couples do it successfully all the time."

"Maybe. If they're focusing on their relationship and not their careers."

"My career is my life. And you had a career, too."

"I'm not the one who left." He stopped in the middle of the boardwalk, then waited for her to turn to face him. "That is why you left, right? Your career?"

She nodded.

"And that's why you came back, too."

Her lips pressed together, but again, she nodded.

"Seems like I'm always getting sloppy seconds." The anger he wanted to hide edged into his voice and he fisted his right hand, trying to tamp it down.

"I told you why I came back." Brusquely, she swiped a lock of hair behind her ear. "I haven't kept any secrets from you, Ken. You know exactly why I'm here."

"You're right. And you know exactly what I want."

"I thought I did." She looked around the pier, turning a slow circle. "But..."

"What?"

"I—I don't know. I'm confused." She squared her shoulders and continued on before he had a chance to ask what she meant. "I guess I'm unclear if this is one of the places you have in mind for Winston's movie, or if this is where...well, if this is where..." She lifted one shoulder, the blush on her cheeks obvious even in the dim light. "You know."

"Where I plan to seduce you?"

"*If* you plan to seduce me." She sounded almost disappointed, and he had an inkling of how intrigued she was by his proposal. Good. He wanted her intrigued, wanted her interested and willing and ready for him...when *he* was ready.

She swallowed, twisting her hands in front of her.

"This place is more sweet than hot. I don't think it's seduction territory."

"You don't?"

When she looked up at him, he thought he saw sadness in the depths of her eyes. "We came here for our first date, Ken. It's a wonderful place, but I don't think of it as sexy. It's special, but it's sweet."

"I'm not sure I agree." He moved toward her, closing his hand on her shoulder when she tried to take a backward step. "I don't think we've explored its full potential."

She squinted, wary. "What do you mean?"

Combing his fingers through her hair, he bent, breathing in the clean smell of her skin. "For example," he whispered, "have you ever made love on a Ferris wheel?"

HIS WORDS BLAZED a path of goose bumps down her spine, leaving a trail of heat in their wake. "I, um, no. I can't say that I have."

"Maybe it's something we should try."

Her head was spinning, and she certainly wasn't thinking about Winston or her job. Instead, she was about to dissolve into a puddle of mush, simply from the caress of his words.

Running her hands through her hair, she turned and wandered to the edge of the pier to look out over the ocean toward Pacific Palisades, grateful he took his hand off her shoulder and let her go. This wasn't Ken, not the Ken she knew. He was playing some kind of game. Earlier, he'd been nothing but sweet and innocent. Schoolboyish, almost. A few hours later and he was practically Barry White, seducing her with his voice. And doing a damn good job of it.

She closed her eyes, annoyed with herself. Of course he was playing a game—he was playing it with *her*. And from what she could tell, he was winning. Certainly if the goal was to make her quake and tremble and imagine his hands running over her body, he'd already won the grand prize.

She heard him move up behind her, then closed her eyes as his hand slid around her waist. "What do you think?"

"About what?" she asked, stalling.

"The Ferris wheel." He bent until she could feel his warm breath tickling the back of her ear. "Shall we give it a try?"

She must have said yes, because the next thing she knew they were standing in line and the operator was holding the door to the bucket open for her. She stepped in, automatically steadying herself on his arm when the bucket swung from her movements.

As soon as she was seated, Ken sat next to her, and although she could have sworn the bucket was wide enough for both of them, he was practically on top of her. His leg brushed against her, and the point of contact suddenly seemed like the focal point of the entire universe. He rested his arm on the back of the seat, his fingers dangling down to tickle her shoulder. He seemed to be touching her all over, stroking and caressing her, and yet in reality, the only contact between them was one tiny spot on her leg and his fingers on her shoulder.

She swallowed, trying to gain control of her senses. No use. She was hyper-aware, and Ken had become the center of her world.

Next to her, he shifted, and her leg grazed his khakis from hip to knee. Though not blatantly erotic, she'd never been more aware of a simple caress, never so in tune with the movements of her body.

Part of it was because it had been so long since she'd been with a man. She'd avoided dating after Tyrell, telling herself she was content to throw herself into trying to salvage her career. So now the sensations…the way her body warmed and tingled…both enticed and thrilled.

But it was more than just the touch of a man. It was the touch of *this* man. Ken. The man she'd wanted so desperately all those years ago.

She hadn't dated in part because of her career, but in moments of honesty she had to admit that she held back partly because she knew she'd never meet another Ken. How could she? She'd had him…and she'd walked away.

And now…now the thrill of having him sang through her veins. She'd wanted his touch—no matter what the price—and so she'd agreed to his condition.

But something was different. She'd agreed to his proposition not just because she needed help, but because she knew Ken. He was safe. But this man— this Ken—wasn't safe. He was dangerous. And Lisa wasn't sure she knew him at all.

Earlier, when she'd tried on the dress, she'd imagined his hands on her, but she hadn't fully imagined his *presence*. Sometime in the past five years, Ken had become more than just a man—he'd become purely male, so male she could practically smell the testosterone, and damn if she didn't want to drown in it.

The wheel creaked as they moved backward, and she started. He moved his arm from the seat to her shoulder and gave her a reassuring squeeze.

"You okay?"

"I'm fine. I just haven't been in one of these things in a while." The wheel lurched, and she squealed, then flashed him a sheepish look. "Sorry."

The corner of his mouth curved up but, to his credit, he didn't tease her, at least not out loud.

They made half the circle, and ended up at the very top, the ocean spread out behind them, and the lights of Los Angeles in front.

He took his arm from around her shoulder, then stroked her cheek with the side of his hand. "Beautiful view."

"It is," she agreed. When she turned to him, his grin widened, and she realized he wasn't talking about the view at all. "Oh. Thank you. I wasn't sure you'd want to pay me a compliment, all things considered."

"It's not a compliment. I'm just stating a fact. No matter what happened between us five years ago, you are beautiful."

She turned, ostensibly to look in the opposite direction, but really because she didn't want him to see that her eyes had filled with tears. She'd wanted sweet words, and instead she got a backhanded compliment mixed with a subtle jibe.

Not that she should care. If she could make peace with Ken, great. But that wasn't her priority; it wasn't why she was here. She needed to get over this moodiness and to keep her eye on the ball. She had no excuse, *none,* not even PMS. And that made the fact that he turned her blood to fire all the more frustrating.

She sat up straighter, determined to regain at least a little bit of the upper hand. Taking a deep breath, she smoothed her palms over her skirt. "You never did answer my question, you know."

"Didn't I? That was rude of me."

She cocked her head to get a better look, to see if he was teasing. He was, of course.

"What question?" he asked.

"About the pier. About why we're here."

"Right." His smile deepened, and she found herself staring at the dimple in his left cheek. "We were discussing whether or not the pier would make an appropriate location for Winston's movie."

The Ferris wheel lurched, beginning its slow journey around. She gripped the side of the seat, but Ken reached over and closed his hand over hers, loosening her fingers until they were twined with his.

"You think it's too sweet a location." He let go of her hand and rested his palm lightly on her bare thigh. He leaned closer and she felt the tickle of his hair on her forehead. "I consider it my personal responsibility to the film industry to convince you otherwise.''

''Ken...'' She squirmed, sure she knew what was coming and scared to death of it. Scared, because she wanted it.

''Shh-hhh...''

He traced his fingertip from her knee up to the hem of her skirt, leaving a trail of heat that pooled between her thighs. With his palm cupping her leg, he stroked the soft flesh inside her thigh with the pad of his thumb.

The gesture was casual, but the effect on her was anything but. Stifling a moan, she fought her body's urge to spread her legs in silent invitation. She wanted him, Lord, how she wanted his hands all over her. But this was his game, and she wasn't admitting defeat that easily—at least, not if her self-control held out. A possibility that, right now, seemed slim at best.

His grazed his thumb up under her skirt, and Lisa's control slipped further away. Though barely beneath the hemline, the movement was erotic in its boldness. ''Open your legs for me.'' His voice teased her senses, setting the tiny hairs on the back of her neck to stand up.

''I...''

''Don't even think about arguing, sweetheart.'' The words were whispered and soft, but there was no mistaking the edge to his voice, and Lisa shivered, wondering what she'd gotten herself into.

Part of her wanted to hold out, to make him beg for her, but something in his voice counseled against it. And besides, she needed this, *wanted* it, and with a moan that started deep in her throat, she shifted in the seat. She spread her legs just slightly, enough to feel the cool air against the heat of her skin, enough to be a clear invitation.

"That's my girl." His voice, rough with need, seemed to fill her senses, making her head spin even as the Ferris wheel sent them up toward the stars. She wanted to follow. Wanted to lose herself in the stars with him.

Her hand closed on the side of the bucket, her fingers tight against the cool metal as she strained against the desire that was filling her. His fingers stroked and played along her skin, his heat filling her as he explored higher and higher.

When his fingertip dipped under the elastic band at the leg of her panties, she groaned and stiffened, terrified of losing herself to the sensations raging through her, and just as terrified not to.

"Tell me you're mine for the night. For anything and everything." His fingers explored her body even as his words wreaked havoc with her head.

"I—"

"Just say it."

"I'm yours." She exhaled, terrified of giving in so easily to this man who was and wasn't Ken. And yet she had no choice. She needed him and she wanted him. And it didn't get any simpler than that.

"Good girl." His lips brushed the top of her ear. "Just relax."

"Easy for you to say," she murmured, tilting her

head back to look at the stars as their bucket once again topped the wheel.

His low chuckle seemed to vibrate through him, and she realized she wanted his laughter almost as much as she wanted his touch. She was losing herself and it terrified her, but not enough to beg him to stop, not enough to make it end. She hadn't been with a man in years, and the pleasure of melting under his touch was too delightful—too forbidden—to turn away from.

Wanting more, she stroked her hand up his leg, thrilled when she reached the telltale bulge that told her he was just as turned on as she was.

"No, you don't." His fingers closed over hers, and he gently moved her hand away, ignoring her murmurs of protest. "This isn't about me."

"Isn't it?" she whispered.

He laughed, soft and low, and the sound made her weak. "Maybe a bit, but we're concentrating on you right now."

The Ferris wheel halted, leaving them suspended two buckets above the ground, the ride was about to end even though the ride she really wanted had barely even begun. Through a haze of need, she turned to look at him and saw longing in his eyes. Passion, and something unrecognizable. A heat, but not the heat of desire. "Ken, please." Her voice was raspy, unrecognizable. "What do you want?"

His warm palm cupped her face, and she turned to rest her cheek in his hand, her eyes never leaving his. "Isn't it obvious?" he asked, his voice just as rough as hers. "I want you. I want you wanting me."

8

DURING THE ENTIRE drive back to the Bellisimo, there was never a moment when he wasn't touching her. Little caresses, a brush of her cheek, his hand resting lightly on her thigh. And every tiny movement, every slight caress, ratcheted her already overwound libido even tighter.

Only when the valet at the hotel opened her door did he slide his hand from her thigh, the gentle movement leaving an indelible imprint on her flesh. She eased herself out of the car and stood by the revolving door hugging herself while he took the valet ticket.

She knew what would happen next—they'd go upstairs, flirt a little more, and end up making love all night. She should feel like a slut. After all, they weren't dating anymore. She was only here with him, letting him stroke and caress her, because she needed something from him. What had he said? Quid pro quo.

But damn if she didn't want the quid, too.

Finished with the car, he came to her and immediately slipped his arm around her waist. "Ready?"

"Sure. Do you want to grab a drink in the bar?"

He brushed her hair aside and pressed a light kiss

against the back of her neck. "Wouldn't you rather go to your room?"

Oh, yes. Trying for casual, she shrugged lightly. "Sure. If you want."

His dimple made a brief appearance as he took her arm, and she was reminded once again of how damn handsome he was. "I want."

"Well, then, by all means, lead the way."

With his arm around her waist, they headed for the elevators, fighting the conventioneers, now dressed in evening clothes. They stepped onto the elevator with a well-dressed group that got off at the next level, probably heading for dinner at Oxygen.

"Are you sure you don't need to check in?"

"That's the beauty of hiring excellent managers. My restaurants run like clockwork even when I'm not there."

"And that doesn't make you feel extraneous?"

They were alone in the elevator, and he turned to stand right in front of her, his palms rubbing softly against her arms. "I find ways to keep busy."

She raised an eyebrow. "Mmm."

The air between them sizzled as he stepped closer, near enough that she could feel him against her, could tell that he was just as aroused as she was. It was an empowering feeling. She wasn't calling the shots—not by any stretch of the imagination—but at least she had this tiny bit of control.

"Have you ever made love in an elevator?" His whisper swept over her, tickling the hair near her ear.

"I thought you were into Ferris wheels."

"Motion," he said, demonstrating by pressing his hips closer still. "Maybe I just like motion."

"I—" She broke off with a gasp when his hand snaked down her back, under the waistband of her skirt, and rested at the swell of her backside. He was crossing the line, and she stood up straighter, almost unwilling to believe Ken was seducing her on an elevator. But the evidence was right there, touching and teasing her. "Ken. Not here."

"Yes, here." His fingers teased her, dipping beneath the band of her bikini-style panties. "You said anything and everything." He cupped her rear, stroking and teasing as her knees went weak and she held on to the handrail for support. "Did you lie?"

"N-no." Someone else's voice. Unfamiliar and raspy. But she didn't care. He was winning. Whatever his game was, he was winning. And she didn't care about that, either. She just closed her eyes and drifted, sandwiched in ecstasy between his hand on her rear, and the hard evidence of his arousal pressed close between her thighs.

He thrust his hips forward, his fingers finding her center with the motion. Another thrust, and she swallowed a gasp as his finger dipped inside her, stroking her wet heat as she writhed shamelessly against him, silently demanding more.

"Do you like that?"

"I...yes." The admission would cost her, she was sure, but she certainly couldn't lie, not when he could feel the evidence of her arousal.

His hand snaked around, sliding between them to

touch her from the front, and she moved closer, spreading her legs to give him better access, then closing her eyes and moaning as he touched her in slow, languid circles. He was driving her crazy, and she wanted nothing more than to be swallowed by insanity.

His other hand moved to her breast, his fingers playing over her nipple through her T-shirt. Lost in an erotic haze, she leaned her head back until it was pressed against the cool glass walls of the elevator.

Glass? Her eyes flew open. "Ken!" She tried to wriggle free. "This is a glass elevator!"

A slow grin spread across his face. "So I noticed."

"People can see." She squirmed some more, but only ended up pressed even tighter against him. His fingers dipped lower, stroking and teasing, and she tried to remember what she was so worried about.

"No one can see." He kissed her earlobe, then her neck.

"You're sure?"

"We're above the fifteenth floor. Too much angle."

"Oh. Well." Her mind told her to protest more. Her body told her to relax and enjoy. And since her knees were weak and her muscles limp, her body was probably going to win the debate.

With a *ding,* the elevator glided to a stop and the doors started to slide open. In an instant he was detached and standing a suitable distance from her, doing nothing more enticing than holding her hand. An elderly couple stepped on, and Lisa wondered if she had some telltale sign of a woman who'd almost been seduced in an elevator.

"This is your floor," Ken said.

Blinking, she looked at the indicator. "Oh. Right."

He preceded her out, then took her hand as she led them to her room.

"Well, here we are." She half leaned against the doorjamb, her head against the wood as she looked into his dark eyes.

"So we are." He traced the pad of his thumb over her lower lip. She opened her mouth, drawing him in, tasting him, until he pulled away.

"I should..." She trailed off, then pulled her key card out of her purse. When the door unlocked, she pushed it open, pausing a bit in the doorway to see if he was following.

He wasn't.

"Ken?"

"Good night, Lisa. I'll see you tomorrow."

She almost laughed, then she realized he was serious. "Tomorrow? But I thought...I mean, you said you wanted..." She took a deep breath and tried again. "I thought we had a deal. Your club for, well, *me.*"

"That's the deal, all right."

She smiled, trying to figure out the joke. "But you're not coming in?"

"Not tonight."

Not tonight? They were doing this again? "But..."

"I never said this was a one-shot deal." He tucked a strand of hair behind her ear. "I just said I wanted you. And I do.'' He moved away, two long strides taking him to the end of the hallway. He turned back and smiled, slow and inviting. ''I'll see you tomorrow. We'll do some more...scouting.''

She didn't breathe until he'd turned the corner, and then she slipped into her room and leaned back against the closed door, relieved, angry and very, very disappointed.

THE COLD SHOWER wasn't doing a damn thing.

Ken pressed his hands against the tile, his head tilted down, and let the spray pound him on the back of the neck as the ice-cold water dribbled down his body. *Nothing.* He was still hard as steel and frustrated as hell.

What kind of idiot walked away from a woman so obviously willing to let him into her bed? Apparently his kind of idiot, since he was now several floors below her, trying to ease off a hard-on with a cold shower.

By all rights, he should be thrilled. He wanted her desperate for him, and he had no doubt that she was. He wanted her hot and willing, and she was. The problem was, he was torturing himself along with her, and if he kept it up much longer, he'd probably burst.

Maybe he should just go back up to her room and put them both out of their misery...

Irritated with himself, he reached down and shut off the water, then stepped dripping onto the tiled bathroom floor. Wrapping a towel around his waist, he finger-combed his hair and wandered into the bedroom in search of clothes.

He caught his reflection in the dresser mirror and cast himself a disdainful look. "You're pathetic, you know?" His reflection didn't answer, and he took that as agreement. Barely twenty-four hours into his plan, and already he was looking for a shortcut simply because he wanted Lisa in his bed.

No way. He was going to play this out as he'd planned. There was nothing between them now. Nothing. Over the course of the evening some of the rough edges of his anger had been smoothed over. But that didn't mean his heart was healed. And he certainly wasn't going to fall under the illusion that some mythical closeness had developed between them simply because they'd had a pleasant evening and she'd melted in his arms.

She'd hurt him, and he now intended to go through with his plan to make a clean break. Flush her out of his system for good. And if that meant making them both horny as hell, then so be it.

Right now he had other things to worry about. He wasn't seeing her again until tomorrow night, and already he missed her. But when he did see her, he needed to be ready. He'd promised her a tour of Los Angeles's most sexy locations, and if there was one thing Ken was certain of it was that Lisa would call the entire bargain off if he didn't keep up his end of the deal.

He pulled on a pair of sweatpants and a ratty U.C.L.A. T-shirt, then wandered around his suite trying to find Tim's magazine. No luck, and he finally remembered that he'd left it downstairs in his office. He glanced at the clock. Almost midnight, and the restaurant closed at ten on Sundays. Chances were good Tim and the rest of the staff would have already locked up, and he could get in and get out without having to face Tim's interrogation.

He managed to get into his office without incident, but soon realized he'd been a little too optimistic about being alone.

"Looking for this?" Tim leaned against the door, waving the magazine.

"Actually I am. I thought you'd already memorized that issue."

"Oh, I have," he said, striding into the room. "Did you know that you can save money on cosmetics by using your lipstick on your cheeks and eyelids? That way your blush is coordinated with your lips and eyes."

"Amazing. And here I've been dumping all my money into eyeliner." He grinned up at his friend. "Seriously, what are you doing here?"

Tim folded himself into a chair. "Thought I'd get an update on your game plan."

Ken chuckled. "My game plan? What the hell are you talking about?"

"The seduction of Lisa, of course." He tossed the magazine onto the desk. "How'd it go tonight and what's on the agenda for tomorrow?"

"You really think I'm going to tell you?"

"Hell, yes," Tim said. "I'm your best friend."

At that, Ken laughed outright. "Can't argue with that."

"Seriously, how'd it go? Like old times?"

Ken could tell from Tim's smile that the question was lighthearted, but even so, it gnawed on him. In fact, the evening *had* seemed like old times, and that was what was frustrating him. "It's not ever going to be like old times again," he finally said. "Hell, I'm not even sure the old times were as good as I thought they were."

"I didn't mean to tap into a sore spot."

"I know you didn't." He ran his hands through his hair. "She just..." He shook his head, knowing words couldn't express the way Lisa made him feel. Hell, he didn't know himself. In so many ways, she completed him, but he just had to look at her and the pain flooded back.

Frustrated, he rubbed the back of his neck. "Never mind. Right now I need to focus on why I came down here in the first place."

Tim kicked back, his long legs crossed at the ankles in front of him. "And here I thought you just missed me."

"How was business tonight?"

"Booming. We took in about thirty percent more than usual for a Sunday. Looks like your idea to have a lounge singer on Sunday was inspired." He grinned. "But you always are."

"Not always." He grabbed the magazine off the desk, then stood to pace the room. "I haven't got a single inspiration about a location to show Lisa tomorrow.''

"Nothing in the magazine?''

He stopped, looking down at the cosmopolitan women's magazine in his hand. "That's why I came down here—to take another look.''

"Well, don't let me keep you from perusing the fashion ads.'' Tim levered himself up and out of the chair. "Have a good night, boss.'' He cast a glance toward the magazine. "And I hope you find some inspiration.''

Back upstairs in his suite, Ken had to admit he was inspired. He was in bed, the magazine open on his lap. The headline—"Sexy City Nights...Love and Lust in the City of Angels''—didn't do the article justice. The reporter had taken it upon herself to combine the universal appeal of Hollywood with the sensual side of Los Angeles and its surroundings. The result was an article that had more than its share of erotic locations inspired by classics of the silver screen.

He flipped the pages, stopping at a double-page spread of a beach at sunset. Lovers walked hand-in-hand along a beach at sunset, waves breaking around their bare feet. They looked at each other, their expressions filled with pure adoration. On the next page, the lovers were intertwined in the surf—the famous beach scene from the movie *From Here to Eternity*.

He stifled a groan, feeling himself harden as he imagined Lisa with him on the beach, her body soft beneath his. Closing his eyes, he let his head fall back against the padded headboard. He pictured her hand in his, soft and supple, as they walked barefoot along the beach. Her skirt danced in the wind, the soft material brushing against his legs as they moved.

His body burned from the thought of Lisa next to him, *wanting* him. And, Lord have mercy, he wanted her.

Frustrated, he tossed the magazine aside and threw off the sheet, letting the cool air soothe his overheated body. Yes, a tribute to the movie seemed like a fine idea, only he'd have to alter the theme a bit to make it uniquely his. For one thing, as erotic as lovers on the beach looked, he had to wonder if all that sand creeping up their bathing suits would be conducive to a seduction.

Not to mention what the bone-deep chill of the Pacific Ocean would do to his...well...enthusiasm. Of course, that might be a good thing. Maybe he needed to start thinking with his head instead of with other parts of his body.

But no. His libido—along with a finely honed need for retribution—was calling the shots. And as long as he'd gotten on this ride, he intended to enjoy it.

IMAGES OF KEN colored her dreams, so vivid she could feel him next to her, so potent she could smell the musk of his skin. She squirmed, reaching for him, but only finding her pillow. *Damn.*

The sharp buzz of the hotel phone wrenched her from sleep completely, and she grappled for the handset, then mumbled a sleepy, "Hello?"

"Rise and shine, sunshine."

She groaned, letting her head fall back onto her pillow. "I'm three hours earlier, Greg. Call back at noon."

"It is noon."

Throwing back the sheet, she bolted upright, trying to focus on the clock. "Oh, no!" Twelve o'clock, straight up.

"Maybe we should rename you van Winkle." He chuckled. "Wild night last night?"

Not wild enough. "Just tired. Working. Jet lag. The whole shebang."

"Yeah, well, you're working all right. I'm impressed. You've barely arrived in La-La Land and you've already captured the crown jewels."

"Excuse me?"

"The crown jewels. The cherry on the sundae. The pièce de résistance. You know—Oxygen."

"What?" It was a shriek more than a question. "Where'd you hear that?"

"From Winston, of course."

"Oh, no!" She slid out of bed and started pacing, one hand holding the phone, the other alternatively fisting and unfisting. "No, no, no!"

"It's not true?"

"No. I mean, yes. It's true. Well, at least it's sort of true. I mean, it will be true." She flopped back onto the bed. "Oh, hell, this is all messed up."

"What do you mean?" She could hear the frown in his voice. "I thought you told Winston—"

"I told Winston I have a deal. Yes, it's all going

to work out fine. I mean, there's no reason why it won't. I just have to live up to my end of the bargain.''

"The bargain?'' He paused. "What bargain?''

After she told him, she had to wait a good five minutes for him to stop laughing. "Would you calm down? This is serious,'' she said sternly.

"I'm sorry,'' he managed to say between guffaws. "It's just that I guess I was wrong.''

"What do you mean?''

"I figured Ken would just roll over and do whatever you asked. I never figured he'd concoct an agenda of his own.'' Another short burst of laughter erupted. "And such a deliciously devious agenda at that.''

She scowled. "He's not the only one with an agenda, you know.''

"What? Your ingenious little plan to have him help you find other locations for the movie? Come on. Do you really think I'm buying that?''

"I don't know what you're talking about.''

"Don't you? You don't need a chaperone. You could scour Los Angeles and find locations with or without him. Which tells me that the only reason you're doing it with him is because you want to.''

She rolled over against her pillow, sure she was blushing even though Greg couldn't see her.

"I'm right, aren't I? Or are you being so quiet for some other reason?''

He was right, of course, but she couldn't bring herself to admit it.

He chuckled again, clearly enjoying himself. "Because I could help you, if you were just looking for some company."

"Okay! Okay! You win. I want Ken to help. I liked spending time with him." Liked the way she'd felt when he'd touched her and liked the way he'd looked at her. She didn't know what his motive was, but that didn't change the way he made her feel.

"Am I good, or what?"

She laughed. "Don't pat yourself on the back too hard. I asked him to help because I didn't want to be the only one on the hook. It wasn't until last night that I realized..." She trailed off, not sure what she realized.

"That all those old feelings were right there under the surface, just waiting to bubble up."

"Yes. I mean, no." She ran her hands through her hair. "I mean, I'm here to get my career back on its feet. And to do that I need Ken's help. I'm just—" she waved her hand in a circle "—taking advantage of the situation." And she intended to enjoy every minute.

Again he chuckled. "Well, I hope you enjoy taking advantage."

"So what did you mean when you said you could help me find locations?"

"I'm flying in tomorrow."

"No way!" She sat up, thrilled she'd have an ally in L.A. "Why?"

"The company is staging the show in Los Angeles.

I'm coming out until they cast someone for the L.A. show."

"Fabulous!"

"Maybe we can spend a little time together. Unless you're too busy…" He paused, and she could hear the smile in his voice. "Unless you're too busy taking advantage of the situation."

"I can only hope, Greg." She smiled, imagining the decadent possibilities. "I can only hope."

9

"WE'RE DEFINITELY NOT in the heart of L.A. anymore."

Ken laughed, watching as Lisa adjusted the blindfold as they sped through the Malibu Canyon toward the Pacific Ocean miles ahead. "What was your first clue?"

She sniffed. "Air quality?"

He shot her an amused look as the Rolling Stones's "You Can't Always Get What You Want" blared out of the speakers. "Don't dis my hometown. The smog's how we keep our secret. Underneath that blanket of smog is the best city on the planet."

"You don't have to tell me. I love Los Angeles. I can't wait to move back."

That surprised him, and he slowed down, turning slightly to see her face. "I thought you loved New York."

"No." She scowled. "New York is great for a while, but I miss L.A. I miss the mountains and the beach. I mean, where else can you ski on Saturday and go scuba diving on Sunday?"

He turned back to the road, amused. "But you never did."

She sighed. "No, but I should have. I should have done a lot of things." In his peripheral vision, he saw that she'd turned toward him. "I was right here for years and I never knew how great I had it."

He swallowed, his hands tightening on the steering wheel. Was she talking about the city? Her career?

Or was she talking about him?

He couldn't ask her outright, so he asked why she didn't come back.

She didn't answer. Instead she slipped a finger under the blindfold. "Come on. Tell me where we're going and let me take this off."

"No way. Answer the question. And quit trying to peek."

With a grimace, she dropped her hands into her lap, then shrugged. "I was an entire continent away. And I thought I had it so great with Tyrell."

His stomach tightened, but he pushed the feeling away. "But it didn't work out with him."

She laughed, the sound harsh and without humor. "That's the understatement of the century."

"So why didn't you come back then?"

She rubbed her hands down her slacks, then half shrugged. "I was there. It was home. I'd made the decision to go, and..." She sighed, apparently not willing to admit out loud how much she hated to fail. "It's not always easy getting back where you want to be, or getting what you want, for that matter."

Her tone was perfectly normal, no sadness or self-pity. But he knew better, and for the first time he had an inkling of how hard it must have been for her. He knew two things for certain about Lisa. First, once upon a time, he'd loved her. And second, she couldn't stand failure.

Not sure it was the right thing to do, he reached over and took her hand. "Don't worry. We'll get you back home."

Her mouth twitched, and she reached up with her free hand to rub her eye under the blindfold. "Thanks, Ken. I knew I could count on you."

"And you can take that off now, if you want."

"Really?"

"It's beautiful here. I'd hate for you to miss out."

She smiled, then gave his fingers a squeeze before pulling the blindfold up and over her hair. She blinked, then inhaled deeply. "It's fabulous."

He watched as she twisted around, taking in the surroundings as they glided by. Rolling green hills, fresh air, winding roads, and no traffic.

"Recognize it?"

At first she hesitated, then she nodded. "I think so. The Malibu Canyon?"

"Right on the money."

She took a deep breath, then sighed. "I always loved it here."

"I remember."

When she turned to him this time, her smile seemed a little melancholy, and the now-familiar guilt settled in his stomach. He was helping her, true, but he was exacting a price. Fair? Probably not. He should just help her, and let her go on about her life. But he wanted her in his bed, wanted her out of his system.

He'd thought he wanted her to pay, also, but now he wasn't so sure. Considering the twisted-up way his insides felt, he wondered if he wasn't the one paying the price.

But he couldn't walk away. Not now that she was beside him. Not now that he'd seen the passion in her eyes when he'd touched her. No, they both had a chance to revisit their past. A dangerous journey, maybe, but it was one he had to make.

"Anyway," she said after a moment, her voice back to normal. "What *are* we doing here?"

"I like this stretch of road." He downshifted to take a tight curve, enjoying the powerful engine at his control.

"It's breathtaking. But where are we going?"

"I'm pitching a theme. You'll have to wait and see."

"Uh-huh. And what sort of theme are we talking about?"

He tossed her a shocked look. "Genius at work, here. Surely you don't want me to reveal all ahead of schedule?"

She quirked a brow. "Um, yeah. Give it up."

"You're sure? Gonna take all the fun out of it."

Turning in her seat, she crossed her arms and shot him an amused look. "Tell!"

He laughed. "Make me."

LISA TAPPED HER FINGERS in time to the radio, considering his demand. *Make me.*

She bit back a smile, certain she could make him if she tried.

"What are you thinking?" he asked.

"I'm trying to decide."

The corner of his lip curled up. "To decide what?"

"If I should make you."

"Ah. Well, I warn you. I might take a lot of convincing." He reached over and traced the tip of his finger along the back of her hand, leaving a trail of heat in the wake of his touch. "Are you sure you're up for it?"

She slipped her hand away, then reached over and closed her fingers around his thigh, enjoying the way he tensed under her touch. "I'm up for anything you've got in mind."

"Are you?" As he spoke, he closed his hand over hers, and she held her breath as he urged it higher until her hand grazed the unmistakable bulge in his slacks.

She stifled a gasp, surprised by his boldness, even though she shouldn't be considering what he'd done to her last night. He pressed her hand down until there was no doubt at all how much he wanted her.

"Are you really up for anything?"

"Y-yes," she whispered, her voice barely audible. She cleared her throat, not willing to lose this round. "Absolutely," she said more strongly.

He twined his fingers with hers. "I'm glad to hear it."

"So tell me." She leaned over, tracing the edge of his ear with her finger, enjoying the tension she saw in his arms as he tried to maintain his concentration on the road. "Tell me what you have planned."

"All right. You've convinced me." He took her hand, kissed her fingertips, then shot her a look clearly designed to shoot straight to the bottom of her heart. *"From Here to Eternity."*

"Excuse me? We're definitely going to meet up with eternity if you don't watch the road."

He grinned, but kept his eyes on her. "The movie." He dragged the pad of his thumb over her lower lip. "The beach scene."

"Oh." She frowned, her forehead creasing as she tried to organize her thoughts.

He'd turned back to the road, but she could see his mouth curve into a smile. "You don't remember?"

"Of course I do." Except she didn't. She was practically a walking movie encyclopedia and she hadn't the faintest idea what he was talking about. He'd so messed with her head that he seemed to have short-circuited her brain. The name was familiar, and the famous scene was right on the tip of her memory.

"Erotic scene, don't you think?"

"Absolutely," she lied. "Enticing. You did your homework." She turned away, scowling at the passing scenery. They crested a hill, and he steered the car to turn onto the Pacific Coast Highway. Below them, she got a quick glimpse of waves crashing on the rocky shore before the hills once again blocked her view.

Waves. She closed her eyes, remembering. Lovers...a beach...of course!

Then she frowned again. Surely he didn't intend...

"You really don't expect us to..." She waved a hand in the air. "You know...on the beach."

"So you do remember the movie."

She shot him what she hoped was a haughty glance. "Of course. Film's my business. Remember?"

"Silly of me to have doubted you."

She heard the tease in his voice but chose to ignore it. "You didn't answer my question. Beach. Public. Us. Not to mention all that itchy sand."

A deep, genuine laugh erupted from him, and she found herself smiling from the mere pleasure of the sound.

"What? Did I say something funny?"

He took her hand, shaking his head vaguely, and pressed a gentle kiss against her palm. "Not funny, just expected. I didn't think you'd like the sand any more than I would, so I'm improvising on my theme."

"Improvising." She crossed her arms over her chest, her head cocked to the side. "Should I be nervous?" A stupid question. *Of course* she should be nervous.

The voice of the D.J. faded from the radio, and another Rolling Stones's song, "Sympathy With the Devil," blared from the speaker. Ken didn't answer the question, just started humming tunelessly with the song.

"You never could sing."

"And you were never a patient woman."

"Looks like I don't have a choice tonight."

"No, you don't." He looked at her, just long enough to meet her eyes before turning back to the road. "But I guarantee it'll be worth the wait."

When he pulled up a few minutes later in front of a bungalow-style bed-and-breakfast tucked into a secluded cul-de-sac on the Malibu cliffs, Lisa decided he was probably right. The place was absolutely charming, and she followed Ken into the entryway where they were greeted by a smiling woman with a distinct Italian accent.

"Mr. Harper! It is so good to see you again."

He clasped her hand, his smile one of genuine pleasure. "Maria, you look wonderful," he said as they stepped inside. He nodded toward Lisa. "This is the young lady who belongs to the luggage I had delivered earlier."

Lisa felt her mouth drop open, and she concentrated on closing it. "You sent luggage ahead?"

"I just had my assistant bring down a few essentials. Toothbrush. Bathing suit. A typical overnight kit."

"Uh-huh."

His boyish grin amused her, and she just shook her head as she looked around. The house was bigger than it looked on the outside, almost as if it had been designed to *look* like a cottage even though it was *designed* for entertaining. A black-and-white photograph of a woman who resembled Maria hung just inside the entryway.

"A relative?" Lisa asked.

"My grandmother."

"She was lovely."

"This was her hideaway," Maria said, but didn't explain further. Instead, she took Lisa's arm. "I'll show you your room, and you can clean up for dinner."

As Maria led her away, Lisa cast a backward look toward Ken. "*My* room?"

"I'm right next door." She must have looked confused, because a look of pure amusement passed over his face. "Oh. And wear the bathing suit under your clothes. We'll go for a walk after we eat."

"But no swimming for at least a half hour." Maria's face was stern with motherly concern.

"Yes, ma'am," Lisa and Ken said in unison. She caught his eye and they laughed. "I'll see you in a sec," she said.

As Maria led her up the stairs to the cozy room she'd been assigned, Lisa couldn't help but think that this was one of the odder outings she'd ever been on. One thing was for certain—Ken wasn't taking any of this casually. Even if only revenge was on his mind, he was planning it with the meticulous attention to detail she'd seen when he'd put together Oxygen. In a weird way, she was even flattered, knowing that someway, somehow, he was spending so much energy thinking about being with her—no matter what the reason.

"It's okay?" Maria stood in the doorway, her pride in the comfortably furnished room clearly visible.

"It's lovely."

The gray-haired woman smiled. "Check the closet and the dresser. I unpacked your things earlier."

"Thank you."

"And hurry down to dinner. Ken stays here at least once a month, but you're the first young lady he's brought." She beamed, and Lisa wondered if she reminded Ken of his mother. "So tonight I made something extra special."

"I can't wait," she said, meaning it. She realized not only how hungry she was, but that she didn't want to disappoint the woman—or Ken, for that matter. "I'll change and be right down."

Maria and Ken hadn't exaggerated. Maria's lasagna was the best Lisa had ever tasted, and the garlic bread practically melted in her mouth. By the time Maria brought out a decadent-looking Italian cream cake, Lisa had eaten so much pasta she had to put up her hands in protest.

"I couldn't eat another bite."

Ken pushed his chair back as well. "Same for me. It was wonderful, though, as usual."

"I'll leave the cake in the kitchen. You two can have dessert later after your walk." She beamed at them, and Lisa had the distinct impression the woman fancied herself a matchmaker. "Now I'm going up to my room to catch up on some reading. You're my only guests tonight, so you've got the entire downstairs to yourselves."

Ken stood as she left the room, then extended a hand to Lisa.

"Are we going outside so soon? I wasn't kidding about being stuffed."

"Then let's sit in here for a bit. Besides, it's still early. Let's let the stragglers clear off the beach so we can have it to ourselves."

She smiled, realizing how nice his proposition sounded.

"In the meantime," he said, "what do you think of Maria's place?"

"It's fabulous."

"For your movie, I mean." He held his hand out, and she took it, then followed him into the den. A fire burned in the fireplace, and he led her to a flowered love seat perfectly positioned to view the flames. He urged her down onto the seat next to him, his arm slipping around her shoulders. "I think it's very, very sexy."

"Well, yes, I see what you mean." She was breathless, her pulse racing. The combination of dim lights, crackling fire, and the man beside her was working on her like a drug, and she wanted to succumb, wanted to lose herself in his arms.

With her next breath, she found his lips on hers, and she opened her mouth, inviting him in. His mouth, hard and demanding, played against hers, coaxing and urging until she found herself melting in his embrace.

His tongue sought entrance, and after granting it, she explored his mouth. He tasted of red wine and heat, and she delved deeper, wanting to consume and be consumed. Wanting to forget their past and lose herself in their present.

His hands stroked her back and shoulders, before moving to the bodice of the sundress and bathing suit she wore. Her breasts swelled tight against the material as her body rose to meet his caress. Tender yet demanding, he plied her with kisses and touches, until she was quivering with need, until her blood ran hot and she couldn't think of anything other than her pure, demanding need for him.

"Ken," she whispered. "Oh, please, Ken."

HIS ENTIRE BODY tightened, his desire for her a physical thing, more pernicious than even the need to eat or sleep. He had to have her, and it took every ounce of strength in his body to pull away.

She looked at him quizzically, a little V appearing above her forehead. Her lips were swollen and red though she wore no lipstick. "What?"

"Not yet," he whispered, gathering his own resolve. "I have something planned."

"From Here to Eternity?"

"Or my version, anyway." He let his gaze drift over her. He'd almost considered stocking her closet with nothing more than a dress similar to the red one she had refused to wear for him. But no—he'd see her in that red dress when the moment was right. And so he'd selected a simple sundress from the boutique on the first floor of the Bellisimo.

The color of the summer sky, the dress was carefree and innocent. His plans weren't innocent, though, and now he traced his finger over the formfitting bodice, thrilling at the peak of her nipple beneath the thin cotton.

"Please," she whispered, her eyes closed.

"Please what?"

She opened her eyes, wide and imploring. "Don't tease me."

His thumb grazed her hard nipple, and she moaned, leaning her head back and moving ever so slightly closer to his touch. His pulse beat faster, ignited by her open response to him. "Do you think I'm teasing?"

"I don't know anymore. All I know is that I want—" She broke off, her teeth worrying on her lower lip.

His took a ragged breath. She was about to admit she wanted him, needed his touch, his caress. "Want what?"

Goose bumps rose on her arms before she leaned back, rubbing herself as if cold. "Nothing." She shook her head. "I don't know. It doesn't matter."

"It matters to me."

She didn't meet his eyes. Instead she gnawed on her lip as she turned, inspecting the small room. "Are you taking me outside?"

"Maybe I'm taking you to heaven." He tried to keep a straight face, but in the end, he cracked a smile at the cliché that had rolled off his lips. He'd wanted to be serious, to keep her on a sensual precipice, but even more, he wanted her completely comfortable with him. The realization disturbed him, and he frowned, determined to keep his plan at the forefront of his mind.

For a second she just looked startled. Then she laughed, too. Rolling her eyes before nudging him with her shoulder. "I'd forgotten how much of a nut you can be."

"Is that good or bad?"

She took his hand, then inhaled a long breath. "Good that you're a nut," she said. She turned away, apparently fascinated with Maria's hardwood floor. "Bad that I'd forgotten."

He felt beads of sweat erupt on his upper lip. She was standing right there in front of him, looking so much like the Lisa he'd known and loved years before. He wanted to gather her into his arms and rock away her fears, wanted to promise her he'd make it all better.

Mentally, he shook himself. He'd made a promise to himself to not get lost in sentimentality, and that was a promise he intended to keep. If he didn't, he'd be risking his heart. And that was a risk he couldn't afford to take.

"Ken?" She was looking at him, her brow furrowed. "I said that it was bad that I'd forgotten."

He waved a hand as if shaking off moodiness. "I guess it's good I'm here to remind you."

A tentative smile danced on the corner of her mouth.

"Now," he continued, "about that dress." He moved toward her, reaching out to sample the material once again.

She skipped backward, laughing. "Uh-uh. Not until you tell me where we're going."

"All right."

"Really? You're actually going to give me some advance notice?"

He smiled, enjoying teasing her. "A bit." He nodded toward the dress. "Got anything on under that?"

"As a matter of fact, I'm wearing a swimsuit. Just like you asked me to."

"Good girl." He grinned, slow and devious. "Then you're dressed for the occasion."

She cast an exasperated glance toward the ceiling. "That's as much information as you're gonna give me, isn't it?" she asked, unable to keep the smile from her voice.

"'Fraid so." Taking her arm, he steered her toward the back door and into Maria's fabulous backyard.

Ken had met Maria at the opening of his first restaurant in Malibu three years ago. The granddaughter of a silent film star that Ken had never heard of, she'd inherited her extravagant home on the beach along with a tidy trust fund. She didn't need money, but she did need company, and so she'd converted the house into a bed-and-breakfast.

Ken had gotten into the habit of coming down at least every couple of months to walk along the beach and relax by the pool. So far, he'd kept Maria's place a secret, not sharing it with anyone. But somehow, he'd wanted to share it with Lisa. It was his oasis, his place to get away from it all, and damn, if he hadn't wanted to escape with her.

Now, though, he wasn't certain he'd made the right choice. This was the kind of place a man brought a lover, not a…whatever Lisa was to him these days.

Part of him considered turning around, getting back in the car and taking her to the next place on his list, deep in the heart of the city. But when she tugged on his hand, her fingers closing around his, all doubts faded.

"This is amazing," she whispered. "It's like a fairyland."

He took a deep breath, realizing that no matter what else, right then he was completely happy. "It is, isn't it?"

Maria's home sat perched above the ocean, with access to the beach from a well-preserved cliffside spiral staircase. The view itself was lovely, but Maria's backyard gave it a run for its money. A customized swimming pool stole the focus of the yard. Deep at one end, the far end sloped toward the ocean, allowing a bather to lie half in and half out of the shallow water. Electronic gadgetry created a wave effect, making it the perfect place to make love in the surf—without the sand and freezing water of the Pacific.

Lisa nodded toward the pool, her expression knowing. "Your plan?"

He grinned, taking her hand to lead her to the far side of the yard. "Something like that."

The pool was surrounded by a hardwood deck. Potted plants filled every nook and cranny, giving the yard the delicious odor of spring. Above, tiny white lights, strung through the branches of the surrounding trees, twinkled in unison with the stars. Lisa was right; it was a fairyland.

They were standing next to the railing, looking down at the surf as it crashed against the beach below.

"Let's go down," she said.

"I drive all this way to find a suitable substitute for sand and cold water, and you want to go down anyway?"

Her eyes danced in the light, and his heart twisted at seeing how happy she looked. "Absolutely."

"Then by all means."

Though stable, the stairs were vertigo-inducing, and he went first, walking half backward so he could keep hold of her hand. She didn't protest, and that merely ratcheted his happiness up another level.

When they reached the beach, she threw her arms out and twirled, her skirt flaring, her face alight with laughter. "It's beautiful here! I've missed the beach so much."

She laughed, her cheeks turning pink, and he was surprised by how much the sound delighted him. He wanted to stay angry, but the more time he spent with her the duller the edge on his anger became.

She took his hand and tugged him toward the water, while he stood his ground in mock protest.

"That water's cold!"

Slipping out of her sandals, she urged him further toward the breaking waves. "Wimp."

Thoroughly amused, he tilted his head back, imploring the heavens. "I went out of my way to find a nice, warm pseudo-ocean, and this is what I get for my troubles.''

She danced around in front of him, her eyes bright as she caught his gaze. An impish grin played on her lips. ''I don't want pseudo-anything.'' Her voice pitched lower and she dropped her eyes. ''I want the real thing.''

When she looked back at him, she was smiling shyly, her eyes darting away, unable to hold his gaze.

His pulse beat an unsteady rhythm, and he licked his dry lips. What was she saying? Was she talking about sex, or more? He didn't know, not for certain, but he sure as hell intended to find out. ''Come on,'' he said, more brusquely than he intended. ''Let's explore the beach.''

''My thoughts exactly.'' Her voice was low, sultry, and his body reacted immediately. He suddenly realized exactly what was happening. Lisa had turned the tables on him. His Lisa, who hated being in the dark about anything, was trying her hand at seduction.

He grinned. If she was so desperate for him she was willing to seduce him, then he'd already won. And damn if he didn't look forward to claiming his prize.

10

HE'D BEEN KEEPING her off-kilter, and Lisa intended to turn the tables. Though considering her body's reaction to an imaginary Ken, she had to wonder if her plan was such a brilliant idea. But she had no intention of turning back. None. He'd said he wanted her. And he was damn well going to get her...even if forcing the issue was a huge mistake.

"Lisa?" He was watching her, his expression hesitant.

With a quick nod of her head, she gestured toward the beach. "Come on." She grabbed his hand and tugged, urging him toward the water's edge.

"This is the Pacific, you know. The water's damn cold."

"Really?" Gathering her courage, she took a deep breath and stepped toward him, until she was close enough that the hem of her dress brushed against his clothes. "Then maybe we need to do something to keep each other warm."

She didn't see him stiffen, but somehow she knew that he had. Trying for sultry, she looped one arm around his neck, stepping nearer to close the tension-filled space between them. The position felt awkward, not right. And for the first time, she realized how much they'd lost when she'd left for New York.

In the past, they'd fit together perfectly. Their eyes only needed to meet and she'd known what he'd been thinking. His finger had only to touch her and she'd melted. Never in her life had she shared such intimacy with another person, and she'd thrown it all away to chase rainbows.

She'd screwed up, maybe permanently. And nothing she could say or do would ever make it better. But, oh, how she wanted to try.

Sagging, she leaned against him, pressing her face against his shoulder.

"Hey, hey. Shh." His arms closed around her, safe and comforting, and she realized she was crying. She sniffled, but didn't pull away. His arms were tight around her waist, her body pressed up against his chest so she could draw on his strength. It felt wonderful, and a silly little part of her wished she could stay that way forever.

Slowly, soothingly, his hand rubbed her back. "You okay?"

She nodded. "I'm fine," she mumbled.

And the truth of it was, she *was* fine. Right then, being held by him, she didn't think anything in the world would faze her. And what had felt awkward and odd only moments ago, now felt like the most right thing on earth. His strong arms encircled her, pulling their bodies together. They fit perfectly, as if they'd been designed for each other. Her arm, which only moments ago had felt heavy and strange around his neck, now urged him closer. Her fingers explored the back of his neck, teasing the short hairs at the base of his haircut. Each touch seemed right, as if she'd touched him this way five years ago...and every day since.

She needed his kisses, needed his heat, and she rose on tiptoes to close her mouth over his. He responded instantly, opening his mouth for her. His hands eased down to cup her rear, urging her against him with one quick pull.

Her body was nearing the melting point, and she was certain that if he let go of her, she'd simply collapse on the sand.

He pulled away, taking the heat that now flowed through her veins with him.

"No." Barely a murmur, her voice pleaded, even though her saner side told her to pull herself together. Right then, she didn't want sanity. Instead, she wanted to be lost in the maelstrom with no cognitive thought. She wanted simply the moment. Simply Ken.

His arms tightened around her waist, but that wasn't enough. She wanted more. Wanted to feel him against every inch of her. Wanted *him.*

His lips grazed her ear, sending little tremors scurrying down her back. Moaning, she tilted her head, inviting him to continue the sweet torment. He accepted the invitation like a gentleman, his mouth moving down her neck.

"More," she whispered. She twisted in his arms, wanting to explore his mouth. But she moved too fast, and they tumbled down into the sand and surf.

Suddenly she was on her back, Ken poised above her, his eyes dark with undisguised lust. And just as suddenly, Lisa wondered what exactly she'd gotten herself into.

SHE WAS RIGHT THERE, close enough to kiss. And Ken intended to do exactly that.

Cold water tickled his feet as the surf rolled in. The hems of his khakis were soaked, and he was sure that Lisa was just as wet.

But she wasn't complaining. Instead, she was looking up at him, eyes wide and inviting.

"Your theme," she whispered.

"Yes, it is." He lowered himself to her. "Eternity," he whispered, then kissed her.

She seemed to melt against him, fitting perfectly, as if she were meant for no one except him.

Her lips were soft and swollen, still ripe from his earlier kisses, and now he teased her mouth, tasting her lips with just the tip of his tongue.

She laughed, the noise mixed with soft protests as she tried to urge him to deepen the kiss.

"Patience, sweetheart."

"I'm not patient," she whispered. "I thought you would have remembered."

He did remember, and that was one reason why his particular choice of punishment was so apropos. He nipped her earlobe. "Maybe it's time you learned."

"Maybe it's time I took charge."

Before he realized what she was doing, she'd managed to roll over, taking him with her, until she was

on top, and he was lying back on the sand. She strad-
dled his hips, and though he didn't think it was possible, his body hardened even more, simply from the
knowledge that she was right there, her sweet, slick
core pressed right against him. He needed to take it
further, wanted her to know how aroused he was.
Grabbing her hips, he rocked her against him, the
motion sending a frenzied burst of electricity coursing
through him.

"Oh, Ken." Her voice was low and soft with pleasure.

"Do you like that?"

"Y-yes."

"Shall I stop?" He slowed the movement, torturing
himself even as he teased her.

"No!" Her eyes flew open, and there was no mistaking the need he saw deep within. "Don't you
dare," she murmured.

Her honest desire thrilled him, and he smiled, taking her hips and rocking her against him until her
breath was just as uneven as his.

"Better?" he murmured.

"Yes." The corner of her mouth lifted in a shy
smile as she moved her hands to balance on his chest.
His body sang from her caresses. The warmth from
her palms spread through him, despite the barrier of
his shirt.

He grazed his hands up her back, no longer con-
trolling the rocking motion of her hips. Though he
wasn't urging her, she kept it up, writhing against him

in an ancient rhythm as she sought her own release—
her body silently promising to bring his, as well.

Control nearly abandoned him, and he fought the
urge to let go and lose himself in the sweet delight
of her arms. That wasn't what he'd planned, not yet,
and he tried to take his mind off the way his blood
burned by watching her.

Her eyes were closed, her features calm. But the
composed picture was belied by her mouth. Her lips
were parted, and he could hear her unsteady
breathing. Her tongue darted out, then her perfect
white teeth grazed her lower lip. Her face was damp
and rosy, and he thought he'd never seen a more
beautiful sight. She was near to losing herself, and
the knowledge brought him that much closer to the
edge.

This was what he'd wanted—to have her on the
brink of passion, brought there by him and for him.
Now that she was there, though, he didn't want to
torture and torment. Instead, he wanted her release,
wanted to see pure joy in her eyes and know that he'd
put it there.

And, Lord help him, the one thing he'd planned so
carefully, the one thing he knew he needed most—to
get her out of his system forever—was the one thing
he absolutely didn't want.

THE UNIVERSE was about to explode around her, and
Lisa welcomed the frenzy, urging it on with every
motion of her body. Ken's hands stroked her back as
she writhed against him. She was wet and hot, and

she wanted him inside her, filling her up and taking her places they'd never gone before. She wanted *him*, and she realized she always had and probably always would.

Right now, though, she wanted the release. She was so close, right there, and she sucked in air, concentrating on the feel of Ken against her. So close... So very close...

And then she wasn't. Instead, she was on her back in the cool sand, and Ken was straddling her, his body not touching hers. Passion burned on his face, undeniable yet controlled.

"What?" she whispered, both disappointed and confused. "I was—"

"Shh-hhh." He pressed a finger to her lips. "We were getting ahead of ourselves. I have a plan, remember? A theme." His smile was warm but firm. "I intend to stick to it."

"I don't mind a little improvisation." She tried to keep her voice light, to not let him know just how much she'd wanted to lose herself in his arms. He had an agenda, and she'd already revealed too much.

"Come on." He stood, holding out a hand for her to grab. "Let's get cleaned up and then go visit the pool."

"Cleaned up?"

He cocked his head toward the stairs, and she saw the concrete foundation and free-standing shower.

She quirked a brow. "A little good, clean fun?"

"Something like that." He ran his hand down the

side of her bathing suit. "We're both gritty, and your dress has seen better days."

"Can't have that."

She followed him to the shower, then pulled off the sundress and, wearing only her bathing suit, stepped into the spray. "It's warm." Closing her eyes, she tilted her head back, letting the droplets caress her face and trickle down her body.

"Want a little help?" His voice was playful, almost sensual, and she opened her eyes as a gentle burst of warm water from another source sprayed over her chest.

Ken was standing in front of her, holding a water hose, a stream of water gushing onto her breasts. "I thought I could help you clean up some of those hard-to-reach places."

"Uh, oh." She swallowed, then tried again. "I—"

He aimed the water lower, hitting her right between the legs, and she snapped her mouth shut, not at all certain what she could possibly have had to say.

"Shh," Ken whispered. "Close your eyes. Let me get you clean."

Closing her eyes, for the first time in her life she wished she were covered in grime. The water from the hose splashed on her toes, and she giggled, stepping lightly to escape the droplets.

"Too cold?"

"No." The water was warm, and in truth it felt wonderful. She was just wound up.

"Relax," he said. "Close your eyes and keep them closed."

She nodded and tried to comply.

"You've got sand in your hair," he said, and with his words came the warm, light flow of water, dribbling over her head, cutting warm, wet paths down her arms, down her chest, over her breasts. Her body quaked, nearly undone by the exquisite sensations.

"Do you like that?"

"Yes. It's..."

"I know." The water flowed over her lips—he must have been holding the hose sideways so that liquid flowed gently against the sensitive skin of her mouth. Then his lips brushed hers through the flow as he kissed her, deep and wet.

The hose moved away, and then she felt the water snaking down her back, the delicious warmth spreading through her. His kiss deepened, his tongue demanding entrance that she readily allowed.

A moan escaped her as she explored his mouth, tasting him, taking in the maleness, wishing she could surround herself with him and lose herself in his heat. She was wet, a wetness that had nothing to do with the hose.

She tried to pull away, needing the distance before he pulled her over the edge merely from his kisses. But he held her close, his teeth nibbling on her lip, his tongue mating with hers.

Her body was spinning. She wanted to open her eyes, wanted to see the world spinning out of control, wanted to meet his gaze. But she'd promised and so she kept her eyes shut, seeing only the colors exploding in her own mind.

So close, so much need, and she urged her hips forward, wanting him to touch her, wanting him to take her that tiny bit further where his kisses couldn't go. But he stepped back, refusing her silent plea for him to stroke her in secret places, to touch her, to finish what he'd started.

"What do you want?"

"I—I want you. Please, Ken. Please."

He kissed her again, rougher, deeper. She gasped, not from the force of his kisses, but from the shock of the hose between her legs. The stream of water touching her exactly how she'd wanted *him* to touch her. A wave of embarrassment washed over her, but faded quickly as she lost herself to the sensations. So vivid, so astounding.

"Spread your legs," he said, and she did, letting him touch her without touching her.

And then, before she was ready, before she saw it coming, the world exploded, and she arched back against his arm, trusting him to keep her upright. Her chest heaved as she struggled to catch her breath.

"That looked like it felt nice." His soft voice tickled her ear.

She opened her eyes and found him smiling at her, the look of pure male satisfaction unmistakable. "That was…amazing."

"Glad you liked it."

She licked her lips, sated, but still wanting more. "So, back to Maria's now?"

"That's my plan." He rubbed the towel vigorously over his hair, then draped it across her shoulders.

"To whose room?" She asked the question boldly, but her stomach was turning somersaults. She wanted him in her bed—hell, she wanted him in *her*—but she wasn't quite willing to beg for it.

She could read the answer from the look on his face—casual, devious, yet a little sad. "It's still my game, sweetheart."

His voice was firm, almost too firm, as if he were trying to convince himself as well as her. Her eyes welled, and she blinked back tears. Until now, she hadn't fully fathomed the depths to which she'd wounded him. But she knew Ken, knew he wanted her, knew he was enjoying this time with her. But something—pride, anger, revenge—wouldn't let him admit it.

"Ken?" She looked up at him, not certain what she wanted to say. "Whose room?" Her voice was too casual, and she was certain he could hear the tiny bit of hope in her tone.

For a moment she thought he would cave. She could see it in his eyes. Real desire. As much as she did, he wanted to ditch his plan, take her to his room, and make love to her until they were too tired to do anything but phone room service. The thought made her tremble, and she fisted her hands, hoping he'd give in to desire.

But then she saw his resolve fall back into place, and she knew it would be another lonely night. She wanted him, he wanted her. But he'd fight it forever.

Damn.

"Ken?" she asked, sure she already knew the answer.

He nodded. "Our separate rooms."

Her lips pressed together, and she considered the wisdom of arguing. Throwing caution to the wind, she stared him in the eye. "You can't hold out much longer. You want me. And I'm going to be just one narrow hallway away."

"I've resisted temptation before."

"You remember I sleep in the nude."

He swallowed, and she chalked up one point for her on her mental scoreboard. "Well, that should give me something to think about until tomorrow night."

She quirked a brow. "Tomorrow?"

"Our next date."

She nodded. Of course. Another night of exquisite torment.

He moved closer and she could smell the lingering scent of the ocean on his body. "And, sweetheart, about tomorrow?"

She nodded, her mouth dry, her body tingling. "Yes?"

"Wear that damn red dress."

11

"YOU SON OF A BITCH!" Alicia shouted the second Ken stepped through the doors.

She'd been waiting for him just inside the restaurant all morning, her fury building with every second that ticked by.

"Good morning to you, too." He stepped past her, barely sparing her a glance, and that infuriated her even more.

She moved sideways, blocking his path.

With a sigh, he stopped, rubbing his hands over red, tired eyes.

"Long night with the little whore?"

Immediately he tensed. Good. Maybe her guess wasn't far off base.

"What do you want, Alicia?" Ice laced his voice, and she shivered, her nerve temporarily fading.

No. Straightening her shoulders, she pulled herself up to her full height—five foot ten in heels—and looked him in the eyes. "I want to know why I can't film one tiny segment of a talk show in your precious restaurant, but some bimbo from New York flits down here and you offer her the entire place on a silver platter."

"Who have you been talking to, Alicia?"

"I'm a reporter, remember? I never reveal my sources."

Suspicion flashed in those Paul Newman eyes. "Dammit, Alicia, what the hell have you heard?"

"Come off it, Harper. Don't play innocent with me. I know all about your arrangement with the little whore."

"Watch yourself, Alicia." His voice was firm, but his smile was a little too tight, and she knew she'd hit a nerve. Despite her initial fury, she'd never really pegged Ken as the type to go all gaga over a woman who offered herself up as part of a business trade, but considering his frosty reaction, she wondered if that wasn't exactly the case.

The possibility was intriguing, and it certainly had the kind of prurient appeal that attracted viewers. If she could nail Harper on this, Gavin would be thrilled.

After a second he turned away, heading for the kitchen with her on his heels.

"No comment, Kenny?"

"I don't know what you're talking about."

She reached out and grabbed his elbow, stopping him before he disappeared into the kitchen. "Then let me refresh your memory. Winston Miller. Movie. Blond bimbette who struck a tidy little deal with you."

Once again his face was calm, almost passive, and she realized why he'd done so well in the business world. The man could be ice when he needed to be.

A muscle twitched in his cheek. "We don't have anything to talk about, Alicia. I think maybe it's time for you to go."

"Nothing to talk about? I think sex for services sounds like a hell of a story." She held her hand out in front of her face, ostensibly checking her nails. "Just the kind of thing that pulls in those killer ratings."

"There's no story, Alicia."

"On that, we'll have to agree to disagree."

A flash of anger marred his features. "You publish one disparaging thing about me or Lisa Neal, and you'll regret the day you met me."

"Touchy, touchy." And interesting. She'd known Ken for about a year, and she'd never seen him quite this worked up before.

"I mean it, Alicia. Watch yourself." With that he headed into the kitchen, leaving her standing in the dining room staring after him.

She'd watch herself, all right. If there was one thing Alicia was good at, it was making sure her ducks were in a row. And she was absolutely certain there was something up with Ken and the lovely Lisa Neal.

And she intended to find out exactly what that was, even if she had to follow them for a week to do it.

KEN WATCHED HER LEAVE, not relaxing until he was certain she'd left the building. Then he dropped into the nearest chair and rested his head on the table. Dammit all to hell. He'd gone and suggested this foolhardy sex-for-revenge scheme to get Lisa out of his system, and all he'd done was put her in jeopardy.

He banged his fist against the table, wishing he didn't care. Wishing he could take it all back. Hell, wishing he could stop. But they'd gone too far, and he wanted to see it through.

Besides, he wasn't certain Alicia had proof. More likely she was grasping at straws. Only two people knew the full nature of his arrangement with Lisa, and that was him and Lisa. He hadn't said anything...and he couldn't believe Lisa would.

She'd already been embroiled in a drug scandal. Surely she wouldn't have told Winston his exact conditions for opening the restaurant to the crew. She wouldn't risk a sex scandal. Not in Hollywood, where sex sells and the tabloids know it. No, more likely she told Winston that Oxygen was locked in—and Alicia had got wind and jumped to her own conclusions.

And that meant two things to Ken. One, he had a grasping, spurned reporter to deal with. And two, Lisa really did intend to see their deal through to the end.

The second idea thrilled him. The first concerned him. Because an hour ago, Alicia'd only had a theory. But there'd been a look of triumph in her eyes when he'd flinched. Which meant she now thought she was hot on the trail of a story.

He'd have to make sure he watched his back—and Lisa's. The last thing either of them needed was a pissed-off reporter breathing down their necks.

"I CAN'T GET A HANDLE on what he wants." Lisa sipped her Starbucks latte and eyed Greg's reflection in the storefront window they were peering through. She'd just finished giving him a rundown of the last two nights with Ken, and she was hoping for brilliant insight. Or at least a shoulder to cry on. "He's driving me insane."

"What do you *think* he wants?"

She turned, looking at him instead of his image. "I *think* he wants me. But he seems determined to not have me."

"Punishment?"

She shrugged. "Seems so. And let me tell you, it's working."

"Getting a little frustrated, are we?"

"I don't know about *we*, but I'm about to go out of my mind."

"I guess he's giving your libido a run for its money," he said, moving down Rodeo drive to the next extremely fashionable and extremely overpriced boutique.

She fell in beside him. "That's the understatement of the year."

"Is it?" His tone was more inquisitive than playful, and held just a hint of challenge.

She stopped, then waited for him to notice and turn to face her. "What do you mean?"

His face was all innocence. "I don't mean a thing. I'm just wondering if it's really just your libido."

Scowling, she pushed her sunglasses higher up on

her nose, then started walking again. "I don't know what you're talking about."

He matched her step for step. "Maybe it's not just your libido. Maybe there's still something between the two of you."

Her immediate reaction was to deny it. Loudly. Emphatically. But she couldn't, and she ended up shrugging, not sure she was comfortable examining the roller coaster of emotions she'd been experiencing these past few days with Ken.

"Lisa..." he prodded, probably reading her mind.

"It's just...I don't know. I guess I went into this thinking I'd simply do whatever Ken wanted. You know, anything for the cause and all that. Whatever it takes to get a crew into Oxygen."

Greg eyed her quizzically. "I'm not following. Are you saying that's not what you're trying to do now?"

"Not exactly." She frowned, trying to put her thoughts in order. What had started out simple—quid pro quo, as Ken had said—was turning out to be incredibly complicated.

She took another sip of her drink. "I'll still do whatever it takes. Nothing's changed there."

"But *something's* changed."

She nodded, stupidly feeling on the brink of tears. Even now, so far away from him, Ken was in her thoughts, had permeated her being. Turning away, she realized they'd stopped in front of the jewelry store simply called Fred. She stared vacantly into the window, barely even conscious of the incredibly beautiful but too-pricey-for-words diamond-and-emerald choker on display.

In the reflection, she saw Greg move up behind her, his face concerned. She tried to smile, hoping to reassure him silently that she'd be fine. But the truth was, she wasn't sure she would be fine.

"Wanna talk about it?"

"I don't think so." She closed her eyes and counted to ten, hoping to keep some semblance of rationality.

"Lisa…" He propped a hand on his hip and flashed her a typical Greg look. "Come on, girlfriend. This is me. Remember? The guy who helped you survive Tyrell."

She ran her hands through her hair. "It's not you."

"No, it is. Really." He patted himself down. "No alien abduction. No Stepford Greg. It's me."

She laughed, clamping a hand over her mouth as she shot him an annoyed look.

He cocked his finger. "Gotcha."

Shaking her head, she tried to not look as amused as she felt. "It's not you. It's me." A wave of frustration washed over her, and she twirled around, as if the motion would somehow expel the confused jumble of feelings that had been building inside her. "I'm not sure I can explain what I'm feeling."

"Can't?" His look was knowing, and she smiled in response. He really did know her well.

"Maybe not *can't.*" She scowled, trying to find the words. "The trouble is I'm not even sure what I'm feeling."

He grabbed her by the shoulders and parked her on a bench. "So let's figure it out."

"What? Suddenly you're Dr. Freud?"

"Ya." He spread his arms, draping them over the back of the bench. "Seriously. Tell Dr. Greg all about it."

"You're not going to leave me alone until I spill everything, are you?"

"Nope."

She tried to keep her face stern, but a smile kept threatening. "Fine." What the heck. Maybe he could help.

"I know things have changed. I mean, it's been five years—of course they've changed. And I know Ken has an agenda. He's told me as much."

"Sex for services. Sounds like a typical L.A. deal."

She nudged him with her elbow. "Be serious."

He passed a hand in front of his face, his expression changing from comical to expressionless, then back again with a second pass.

She rolled her eyes, but continued. "The thing is, even though he's trying his damnedest to torment me—and doing a good job of it—still, the old Ken keeps poking through the cracks. The Ken I knew. The one who loved me and would never have played games. Who never would have even thought of it if I hadn't hurt him."

"And you're still in love with him."

She pressed her lips together, not willing even to examine that question. "I don't know. It doesn't matter. Even if I am, it doesn't matter. I'm not looking for a relationship right now. I'm focusing on my career. That's not a secret, Greg. Not to you, not to Ken."

"How do you know you can't do both?"

"Because I know *me*." She ran her hand through her hair, thinking of her mom, who could have made millions if she'd never left New York, and her sister, stuck in Idaho snapping pictures of toddlers. "I've got one chance to make up for the whole Tyrell fiasco. One. And I'm not going to blow it. Besides," she added, "whether or not I'm in love with Ken Harper is the least of my problems. My problem is sex."

"Welcome to the new millennium."

"I can see *you're* going to be a lot of help."

"Sorry." His expression shifted to contrite, and she rolled her eyes again. "Really. Tell me about it."

She lifted a shoulder. "It's driving me crazy. It's like every time I catch even the slightest glimpse of the way things used to be, my resolve weakens."

"Your resolve?"

"When he suggested—" she waved her hand in the air "—this whole deal, I didn't hesitate. I mean, I'll do whatever it takes to get access to Oxygen. I have to—my entire career is on the line."

"And you have. So how's your resolve weakening? What's the problem?"

"The problem?" She stood, paced in front of the bench, then sat back down again. "The problem is, he's not lacing his quid with any pro quos."

"You lost me."

"He's just teasing me. He's dangling sex in front of me like a carrot in front of a mule. I keep chasing after it, but I'll never get it." Her voice rose, and an elderly woman coming out of Fred glanced her way. Her cheeks burned, and she studied her hands in her lap.

"But if you only have to do what he wants..."

"I know. *I know.* I *should* be thrilled."

"Ah. But you want to get laid." He took her hand. "And that means you're not thrilled at all."

A renegade tear trickled down her cheek and she brushed it away, feeling like a fool. "No. I'm not."

"You want him."

"So much it sometimes hurts to breathe. And twice now he's left me high and dry."

"So?"

"So?" Her voice squeaked. "So? If this were happening to you, you'd be running around the apartment complaining about blue balls or some such nonsense."

"So, buy a vibrator."

She tried to swallow a giggle. "Oh, thank you. You're very helpful." She glared. "I don't *want* a vibrator. I want—"

She clapped her hand over her mouth, both shocked by the onslaught of desire and fearful another elderly lady had overheard her.

"Look, kid. I'm no expert on male-female relationships, but it seems to me that two can play his game."

"I've tried."

He crossed his arms over his chest. "Honey, considering everything you've told me you two have done, if you haven't managed to actually do the deed yet, then you haven't tried hard enough."

Maybe he had a point. Even though she'd intended to see it through last night, when Ken had called it quits, she hadn't protested. She'd just meekly gone on her way. "I guess I'm afraid that's against his rules."

Greg shrugged. "He said he wanted you, right?"

She nodded.

"And all the evidence suggests he meant it sexually, yes?"

"Oh, yeah."

"And he never actually said he wanted to make you horny as hell and leave you to suffer, did he?"

"Well, he didn't say it to me."

"There you go."

She shook her head. "You lost me."

"If you get him in bed, you're still playing by his rules. If he doesn't want to sleep with you, he should have told you. And if he really doesn't want to, then he can just exercise great self-control." His grin spread across his face. "But if you manage to seduce him, you haven't broken any rules, and you'll be that much less frustrated. I don't see how you can lose."

"Maybe…"

"Trust me." He got up and steered them toward his rental car, parked nearby on the street. "Come on.

We passed a pharmacy. We'll stop in on the way back and stock you **up** on latex accessories.''

"Greg..." she admonished, looking around to see if any of the posh Rodeo Drive shoppers had overheard him.

He clicked a button on his key chain, unlocking the car, then opened the door for her.

"You know," he said as she slid into the car. "You haven't answered the one really big question."

She frowned, afraid that, somehow, she knew what he was going to say. "What question?"

"Is it just sex you want? Or something more?"

He shut the door before she could answer, and she was grateful for the moment alone. He'd asked the one question she'd been avoiding.

And the truth was, she really didn't know.

"KEN HARPER! So good of you to come by. Where've you been keeping yourself?" Oscar Toya, one of L.A.'s wealthiest men with no apparent source of income, pumped Ken's hand. Behind them, the crowd buzzed as it moved en masse through Oscar's elegant foyer.

Ken's arm tightened around Lisa's waist, the smooth silk of that fabulous red dress soft against the sleeve of his suitcoat. "I've been at Oxygen, Oscar." He winked. "Why haven't you?" Oscar was one of his dearest friends, and it had been months since he'd had the chance to sit and talk with the fatherly man.

The older man laughed, then slapped Ken on the

back with good-natured joviality before his eyes turned to Lisa. "Who's your lovely companion?"

"Oscar, I'd like to introduce you to Lisa Neal. Lisa, this is Oscar Toya."

"It's a pleasure to meet you, sir. I've certainly heard a lot about you."

"If you read it in the social pages, it's lies, all lies. If you read it in the financial pages, it's probably a lie—"

"And if you read it in the funny pages, it's nothing but the truth." Emily Toya, looking as elegant as her surroundings, slid her arm through her husband's. "It's an old joke, dear. I'm sure Ken and his lady friend have heard it."

Oscar kissed the gray at his wife's temple. "Lisa Neal," he said by way of introduction. "I haven't gotten around to interrogating the boy yet about their relationship."

Lisa smiled, and Ken stifled a cringe. Oscar was as perceptive as he was wily, and Ken wasn't certain he wanted the man psychoanalyzing him.

"Well, you go right ahead," Emily said. "I'll take Lisa and give her a quick tour of the house."

"We can't stay," Ken said. "I just wanted to stop by and wish the two of you a happy anniversary. I'm sure the party will be a huge success."

Lisa squeezed his hand. "Actually, I'd love the twenty-five-cent tour. Surely we can spare a few minutes while Mrs. Toya shows me around?"

"Emily," she said. "And if Ken says no, I'll have to strike him from my permanent guest list. You stay and talk to Oscar and I'll deliver her back safely in just a few minutes.''

''Can't risk my social standing.'' Ken couldn't help but grin, even though he dreaded imagining what Lisa and Emily would talk about.

As the women walked away, Oscar turned to him. ''I like that one. Not like those fluff types you've brought here before.''

Even though Ken agreed totally, he wasn't about to admit it out loud. ''You talked with her for two seconds. How could you possibly get a feel for Lisa yet?''

''Instinct, son. I'm right, aren't I?''

Ken exhaled, but didn't answer.

''You don't have to say a word. I see it in your eyes. She's special, and you're smitten.''

''Smitten? What is this? A Mickey Rooney remake?''

''Joke all you want, but I know a man in love when I see one.''

Ken flinched, and Oscar nodded.

''Uh-huh. Struck a chord, I did. Instinct, my boy. What did I tell you?''

''Your instincts are about five years off.''

''Eh?'' The old man cupped his hand around his ear, even though Ken was absolutely certain he'd heard every word Ken had said.

''I loved her five years ago. But things happened.''

''Things always happen.''

''It's not love, Oscar.'' He shook his head, working to convince himself more than Oscar. ''Memories, maybe. Closure, possibly. Lust, definitely. But love? Not her. Not again.''

"Believe what you want, son. But sooner or later you're going to have to face the truth.''

"Oscar...''

His friend held up a hand. "I know, I know. Mind my own business. But I'm an old man, and being nosy and opinionated is about the only perk that comes with that particular territory.''

Shaking his head, Ken could only grin.

"Don't worry. I'm changing the subject. I was reading about you recently.''

"Uh-oh.''

"Nothing terribly revealing, I'm sad to say. Just that profile in *Los Angeles* magazine.''

Ken nodded. He'd consented to the interview because the reporter had agreed to his condition of no cameras in his restaurants. Too bad Alicia and a half dozen other reporters weren't as cooperative.

"Whatever happened to your idea of a diner?''

Ken shrugged, trying for nonchalant. "You know how those things go. It was an idea I had when I first moved out here. When Oxygen took off, it seemed silly to move backward.''

That was only half true. The idea of opening a diner still gnawed at him. He'd always liked the idea of someplace that would get him back to his roots. Someplace folks without a brokerage account could afford and enjoy.

He'd sketched the original design for Lisa on a napkin, and she'd been so enthusiastic he'd registered the assumed name the next day. But when Lisa had abandoned him, he'd abandoned the idea. Unfortunately, the reporter was more industrious than Ken had anticipated, and he'd located the filing. Ken had told him the same story he was now telling Oscar. Not the full story, perhaps, but the truth was that he had moved on.

"No offense to Tim, but a person can only ingest so much goat cheese and arugula," Oscar said. "I think it's a winning idea."

"What's that?" Lisa asked as she and Emily reappeared.

"Ken's thinking about opening a diner."

"No, I'm—"

"What a wonderful idea," Emily said.

Lisa shot him a quizzical look, but he merely shook his head.

"I want to hear all about it," Emily said.

"Of course," he said, trying to think of a decent excuse, "but—"

"Ken's doing me a favor and promised to take me to a few nightclubs and a rave," Lisa cut in, shooting him a glance.

"A rave?" Oscar's voice was incredulous. "Our Ken? Why are you torturing the boy?"

She laughed. "I'm scouting locations for a film. He's helping."

"To help you with a task like that he's one hell of a nice guy," Oscar said. And then, when Lisa turned to clasp Emily's hand, he mouthed to Ken, *Or a man in love.*

LISA WAS BUCKLING her seat belt when Ken closed his hands over hers, squeezing lightly.

"Thank you," he said.

Lisa turned to face him better in the car. "For what?"

"For getting me out of there." His eyes flashed warm and playful. "And also for wearing that dress."

Liquid heat pooled somewhere between her thighs. "You're welcome." She worked to keep her voice steady. "But it wasn't just for you. You *do* owe me a night on the town. So far I've got two locations and you've still got to put out."

His sexy smile rocketed straight to her heart. "Don't worry about that, babe. I intend to put out." He reached over to tease the back of her neck with the tips of his fingers. "I'm just waiting for the right time."

"Mmm-hmm." She hoped she sounded nonchalant, but she probably sounded overeager. More than just the physical, she was enjoying every moment she spent with Ken. He'd changed, true, but the old Ken was still around—the one who made her laugh even as he tried to torment her. And the new Ken—the Ken who could reduce her to shakes and shivers with nothing more than a look—well, that Ken was damned appealing, too.

She took a deep breath and settled back into the seat. "So, where are we going?" she asked, trying to keep a straight face. It seemed that every time they got into a car, she was asking that very question.

"We're going to go scope out enemy territory, then

find a rave party, and then we're off to a little surprise.''

"'Enemy territory'?''

"Other restaurants. Nightclubs that compete with Oxygen and my other spots.''

She clasped a hand over her heart. "Why, sir, I'm honored. To think you'd face the enemy for little old me.''

He turned to face her long enough to wink. "For a beautiful damsel, of course. And, also, I'm always happy to have an excuse to scope out the competition.''

Laughing, she squeezed his hand, totally at ease with him. A haze of desire still filled the air, but it wasn't as stifling or uncomfortable. Instead, it was welcome. She wanted him, he wanted her and, in the meantime, she was having a fabulous time just enjoying his company.

As it turned out, the competition was pretty darn competitive. Each of the hot spots they visited seethed with atmosphere. Some had dim lighting and secluded tables, others were modern and trendy, with a crush of bodies and the sensual thrum of music. Though Lisa didn't think any of the restaurants and clubs they visited held a candle to Oxygen, it was almost like old times, with her on Ken's arm as he steered her from one establishment to the next.

Two of the restaurants seemed perfect for scenes in Winston's script, and Ken introduced her to the owners. She'd taken their phone numbers and re-

ceived a semifirm commitment to cooperate with the
filming in exchange for a film credit.

Overall, the evening was a whirlwind, and when
they ended up in a corner booth in an Art Deco restaurant just off Sunset Boulevard, she collapsed grate-
fully into the cushioned seat, letting the swing sounds
of a live big band surround her. "This has been fabulous. I'm exhausted, but it's been wonderful."

He slid into the seat opposite her, then reached
across the table to take her hand. "Glad you approve
of my scouting attempts."

"I hope you keep it a secret," she teased. "If you
tell Winston, he'll hire you and not me."

"Your secret is safe with me." He stroked her
wrist with the pad of his thumb. A simple touch, nothing untoward or unseemly, and yet to Lisa it was su-
premely erotic. Every stroke, every bit of pressure,
seemed to shoot through her, gathering in secret,
wanting places.

"Still want to go to a rave party?"

She frowned, wondering if it was really necessary.
Right at that moment, she didn't want to do anything
but sit in the booth and hold hands with Ken—which,
of course, only proved that she wasn't cut out for a
career *and* a relationship. Balancing life and work
wasn't her strong suit, and she didn't intend to make
short shrift of her career.

"I didn't realize it was a trick question. Congress
usually takes less time to decide."

"Sorry." She tried to pull her hand away, but he

held fast. "I didn't realize... No. I don't think we need to go to a rave."

"You're sure?"

"Why? Do you want to go?" Somehow the image of Ken wandering among boozed-up twenty-somethings slithering across a dance floor didn't quite fit.

"To the party? No." With the tip of his index finger, he traced his way down the back of her hand. "But to dance with you..." His voice trailed off, the invitation clear.

She took a deep breath. If she couldn't have him back in her life, she intended to have *him*. "All right."

"Excellent." When he slid from his seat and held out his hand for her, she had second thoughts.

"You do remember I can't dance worth a darn?"

"Nobody will be watching."

"You will."

His soft smile just about melted her heart. "I'll be impressed no matter what you look like on the dance floor."

The band started playing a Glenn Miller tune as they arrived at the polished floor. Couples bopped in time to the music, swinging out and back with movements that looked choreographed.

"I don't think I can do that."

"Sure you can. It's just your basic swing. They're mostly doing the Lindy Hop."

She squinted, wondering what planet he was from. "And you know this because..."

He chuckled, then cocked his head toward the dance floor. "I've got a big band and a dance floor in my Orange County restaurant. I love swing."

"I never knew."

"There's a lot about each other we never got to know."

She looked up, wanting to see if she'd imagined the criticism in his voice. But he was only smiling and urging her forward.

"It's easy. Your basic eight steps." He demonstrated while she stood there like a lump. He looked so sexy the way his body moved in his loose khakis and sport coat that she really couldn't do anything but stare. "Got it?"

She nodded dumbly.

They tried together, but she managed to trip over first her own feet and then his. She knew her cheeks had to be bright red, and she hoped everyone in the club wasn't staring at her.

After a few more fumbling attempts, he gave up, holding her at arm's length. He was laughing, and his eyes were dancing, so at least she knew she hadn't destroyed his evening.

"I told you I couldn't dance," she said.

"And you didn't lie." He kept his voice perfectly serious, but the twitch at the corner of his mouth revealed his amusement.

"Mmm." She frowned. "Take pity on me? Take me back to the booth and buy me another drink."

"I've got a better idea."

Before she knew what was happening, he gathered

her into his arms and started slow dancing, swaying not in time to the music, but to some rhythm that was only between the two of them.

"Ken, people will—"

"Shh."

She almost protested more, but it felt too good to be in his arms. Instead she pressed herself against him, letting him rock them back and forth.

"I can't believe I'm in lo—" He stiffened, and she stifled the urge to look up, to see his face and know what he was thinking. He cleared his throat. "I can't believe I was once in love with a woman who can't dance."

She laughed, knowing that was expected, and wanting to ease the moment. But her face was still pressed against his chest, and she frowned, wondering which was real—what he'd started to say or what he'd actually said.

And if he did still love her...what on earth was she going to do now?

12

THEY DANCED for what seemed like hours, Lisa pressed against him, exactly where he wanted her to be. Only when they finally flashed the lights, indicating that the club was closing, did she leave his arms.

Now they were heading together toward his car, Lisa bouncing in front of him.

"That was great fun," she said, doing a little twirl.

He laughed. "Oh, sure. *Now* you dance."

"I danced with you." Reaching out, she brushed the lapel of his jacket. Then she seemed to realize what she was doing, because she jerked her arm away, her gaze darting to the sidewalk as she turned to face forward.

She was everything he'd remembered and more. Warm, ambitious, funny. A woman he could talk to. The *only* woman he could talk to who set his body on edge. He had women friends, sure, but none whom he wanted to strip naked and sink deep inside.

And he'd been with women who'd made him hard as steel, who'd made his blood burn and his pulse race. But with them, sex was all he wanted. Lounging about, talking or laughing, seemed extraneous, even forced.

But with Lisa...with Lisa he wanted the whole package. The wild moments of decadence and the soft, intimate moments. The playful times and the quiet times. Everything. And damn, if that wasn't going to be a problem.

He tensed, mentally urging himself back to rational thought. Their history was pain. He'd gotten over it, true, but that didn't change that she'd hurt him. She'd been young and had career tunnel vision—he could understand; he'd been exactly the same.

The trouble now, though, was that he didn't believe she'd changed. As soon as she locked in her locations, she'd be out of here. He couldn't open himself up to her, not if he wanted to survive. Sleep with her? Sure. And he intended to do just that. But sex was sex and love was love, and right now—with Lisa—love was out of the question.

Sex, however, was very much on the horizon. A good thing, too, since the sight of her moving under that naughty red dress had him harder than he'd been since...well, since their night on the beach. He hurried to catch up, then pressed his palm against her back, delighting in the soft sigh that escaped her lips.

"Slow down, sweetheart. What's your rush?"

She tossed a smile over her shoulder as they stopped in front of his car. "I'm not in a hurry, soldier. I've got all the time in the world."

"Yeah?" With his finger, he traced a path down her spine, thrilled by the little shiver his touch caused. She reached out, balancing herself against the frame of his car as a sigh escaped her. A sigh *he* caused.

Need came upon him with a primal demand, and he pressed up behind her, feeling the soft curves of her rear against him, delicious and enticing. His car was parked in the far corner of the lot, a secluded, dark place. Perfect for a seduction.

"So tell me about the script," he murmured as his hand slid along her bare back to caress the firm side of her breast.

"I, uh, what?"

"The script. What kind of locations?" He kept his voice low, demanding yet soft. "Anything outside?"

His finger flicked over her nipple, and she cried out, pushing herself against him as if she needed the contact as much as he did.

"Any outdoor locations?" he repeated.

"Yes. Oh, yes."

"Are you wearing anything under that dress?"

She nodded.

With his palm, he grazed her nipple, then pressed a soft kiss against her neck when she arched back in response. "You're not wearing a bra. So you must be wearing panties...?"

"Yes." A whisper, barely audible.

"Take them off."

She stiffened, and for a moment he thought she was going to protest. Then she reached up under her skirt and urged her panties down until they fell in a puddle of pink silk around her ankles.

He bent and picked them up as she stepped out of them. As he stood, he trailed his fingers up the back of her leg. She shifted, opening her legs for him, but it wasn't an invitation he was ready for yet.

Instead he nuzzled her neck. "Not here." Reaching around her, he opened the door to the car and helped her inside.

"Where?"

"Soon," he said, then shut the door and walked around the car to the driver's side. The night was cool, but it did nothing to lower his body temperature. He'd been tempted to take her right there in the parking lot. To pull up her dress and sink into her warm, slick heat. He wanted it, she wanted it. Fortunately for both of them, he still had a modicum of self-control.

"Are we going far?" she asked as he cranked the engine.

"Not far."

Her sultry grin warmed him. "Good."

His sentiments exactly.

It took all his concentration to keep his eyes on the road and not on the woman next to him, but somehow he managed. After a few minutes they were on Mulholland Drive heading west, the lights of the city burning below them like pinpricks of light through a black velvet curtain.

When he reached the curve in the road he'd been looking for, he pulled off onto the dirt shoulder and got out of the car.

"Where are we?" she asked when he opened her door.

"Overlook," he said, pointing across the street at

the bench poised at the top of a small hill. "Privacy, and a view."

"Privacy?"

"Absolutely. Nobody driving by's going to look up at that bench."

"Uh-huh."

"Besides, it's almost 3:00 a.m." He slipped his arm around her waist. "Shall we?"

She hesitated less than a second before nodding. "Let's."

They climbed up the hill, following the narrow footpath that thousands of lovers must have walked before them. When they finally crested the hill, Lisa sighed. "Oh, Ken. It's beautiful."

He had to agree. The bench faced the Westside, its back facing Mulholland and the San Fernando Valley. The lights of Los Angeles spread out below them, ending abruptly in the distance where the city gave way to the ocean.

"It's perfect," she said, and he was unsure whether she meant for her movie or for them.

Moving behind her, he wrapped his arms around her waist, breathing in the fresh scent of her hair. "I could stay this way forever," he murmured as she sighed contentedly. It was a lie, though. With every passing moment, his awareness of her grew, and his body burned hot and hard merely from her touch. Forever would drive him crazy. He had to have more of her.

Bending slightly, he caught the hem of her dress in his fingers, then urged it up until he'd revealed the back of her lush thigh that seemed to go on forever. She shivered, a little moan escaping. "Are you cold?" he asked.

She shook her head, gasping when he traced the soft flesh where her hip and thigh met. He was hard as steel, and he pressed close, letting her stroke and tease him with the movements of her firm rear while he did the same to her with his touch.

Like a man seeking treasure, he slipped his hand in front, stroking her coarse, damp curls, then down, further, until his finger was poised just before heaven. He stopped, and she squirmed, her impatient movements thrilling him no end.

"Say it," he whispered.

"Don't...don't stop."

His lips brushed her hair and then the back of her ear as his other hand slipped under the bodice of that wonderful dress. Her nipples were hard, and she leaned forward, silently pleading with him to continue his caresses.

"Don't stop what?"

"What you're doing. Touching me." Her words were breathy, her head tilted back to the stars.

"Tell me what I'll find. Are you wet? Do you want me?"

She took a breath, her body trembling. "Yes. Oh, yes, please."

His fingers dipped low, his own moan coming in unison with hers when he discovered how warm and wet she was. She wanted him, craved him, and the knowledge was intoxicating. He stroked her, teasing and playing, finding her core and moving his fingers in slow, rhythmic motions, then faster and faster until she stiffened in his arms and he knew she was on the edge.

When he stopped, she cried out, begging him to continue, but he simply guided her to the bench, then sat down. He urged her onto his lap, straddling him. He wanted to feel her against him, wanted to see her face as he took her over the edge.

Her wide eyes were dark and pleading, and he knew he couldn't disappoint her. With a fluid motion, he slipped his hand between them, stroking her again as she arched back against the arm wrapped around her waist.

Leaning forward, he closed his mouth over her breast, sucking and teasing through the slippery fabric as she writhed against his hand. Her breath came faster and faster and he knew she was about to explode in his arms.

With a slight tremble, she straightened, her face a mask of intense concentration as she leaned forward to tackle his fly.

"No, no," he said, closing his hands over hers, even though he wanted to rip his fly open and sink into her. "This is about you."

"Please. Oh, Ken, please. I want you."

Damn, but he wanted to lose himself inside her. But that wasn't his plan. Not yet. She was on the edge, true. But his plan was for her to be falling over the precipice, hanging on by nothing more than her fingernails. And his plan was important, even if, at the moment, he couldn't exactly remember why.

But right then, right there, she was warm and willing, and he wanted her. Wanted her more than he could remember wanting anything in his life.

With a guttural moan, he swallowed a curse and nodded. "Yes, sweetheart, I want you, too."

SHE HAD CONDOMS in her purse, and Lisa didn't think she'd ever been more grateful to anyone than she was to Greg right then. Thank goodness he'd forced her to buy some. At the moment she just wished he'd insisted she get the twelve-pack.

She'd promised herself she wouldn't let Ken leave her high and dry again. She wanted him, needed him even, and right now she intended to have him.

"Kiss me," he whispered, and she readily obliged. Leaning forward, she brushed her lips over his, delighting in the way she felt him grow even harder beneath her. She concentrated on the kiss, sucking and teasing, urging his mouth open so she could explore to her heart's content.

A low groan rose from his throat, and she suppressed a secret smile, knowing she was the cause. His hands locked around her hips, rocking her back and forth as they both worked themselves into a frenzy.

"Now," she whispered, and she reached for his fly when he nodded in silent agreement.

When he was free, she stroked him, reveling in the way he trembled at her touch. Faster and faster, she moved her hand over the velvety smoothness, wanting to take him to the edge just as he'd taken her.

His hand closed over hers, stopping her, and she looked up to see his eyes burning with passion. "Now," he said, lifting her by the hips, until she was poised over him, the position teasing them both. She wriggled, wanting more contact, more intimacy, and then he delivered, thrusting her down again so that he impaled her in one fast, slick movement.

"Oh, yes. Ken, yes." Her voice was barely a moan, and she rocked against him, tight around his shaft, finally experiencing what she'd wanted so badly so many years ago. And now that she was here, in his arms, lost in a haze of passion with him, she knew she didn't want to live without his touch ever again.

They rocked together, at first slow and languid, then faster and faster as passion grew. He buried his face between her breasts, suckling and teasing through the thin material of her dress. His hands stroked her thighs, teasing the soft inner skin.

His thumb sought her most sensitive spot, his rhythmic motion keeping time with their primal dance. His touch was like electricity, shooting through her, pooling in her center, but radiating out to her fingers and toes.

"Lisa," he murmured, his voice straining. "Oh, Lisa."

He trembled beneath her, and she knew he was on the edge, just as she was. "Please," she whispered, even as he thrust into her, satisfying her every wish with that one, claiming movement.

The world exploded around her, and she threw her body forward, clutching his shoulders as she tilted her head back. Above them, the stars blurred into a maelstrom of swirling light. His hands around her felt warm and safe, and she curled up against him, her head buried against his shoulder. This man. *Ken.* A man who made her feel things she'd never felt before. She trembled, and his arms tightened.

"Cold?"

"I'm fine," she said, but she wasn't. She was lost, confused. Totally unsure about how she felt about him, or about how he felt about her. She bit her lip, wondering if she was just an object of revenge. He'd almost said he loved her, almost said it out loud. So maybe he did. Maybe he always had.

He pulled her close against him, his arms providing the comfort she needed. Could they go back to what they once had? She didn't know, but right then, right there, lost in a haze of passion, she almost believed they could.

In so many ways she wanted to rejoice, to kiss him, to sing loud and clear, to dance around. But one tiny part of her held back, cold and terrified, certain she'd have to give up everything in order to love Ken.

ALICIA STOOD on the darkened road, a camera with a zoom lens pressed to her face as she watched Ken and Lisa on the bench, unaware as they made love that their little tryst was being recorded for posterity.

Bastard. And the little bitch, too. She'd done her research on Lisa Neal. The woman had thrown away a perfectly good career blowing studio money up her nose with her lover, Drake Tyrell. And now Winston Miller was giving her a second chance. Unbelieveable.

No one had ever given her a second chance; she'd had to scrape and claw for every crumb.

And even more unbelievable, Ken Harper was holding Lisa Neal in his arms. Tasting her, kissing her. And looking for all the world like he enjoyed it.

She watched as Ken kissed the little bimbo, her camera whirring as it took shot after shot. Her temper flared with each passing frame, and she considered climbing the hill to confront the two of them. Lisa Neal didn't belong with Ken. She didn't deserve him.

She held back, of course. She had a plan, after all, and she didn't intend to get carried away and screw up her possibilities.

She patted the camera, a smile touching her lips. Ken Harper would let her into that restaurant, of that she was certain.

"YOU'RE IN LOVE, my friend," Tim announced as Ken hobbled into the office at the crack of dawn.

He ran his hands over his face, rubbing slightly to try to wake himself up. "What are you doing here?"

From his seat at the worktable, Tim shot him a "duh" look. "Inventory. You remember. All the little details it takes to keep this restaurant operating like a well-oiled machine."

"Right. Of course." He shook his head, trying to shake off exhaustion. "Sorry. Not all here yet."

"Long night?"

"Wonderful night," Ken said, knowing he was grinning like an idiot. He'd started out wanting to punish her and ended up wanting to cherish her. His entire plan had flipped one-hundred-and-eighty degrees. Control was like a long, lost dream. Instead, he was spinning out into the stratosphere.

Losing himself inside Lisa had been everything he'd dreamed it would be. Miraculous. Stunning. *Life-changing*. After kissing her good-night at her door, he'd crawled to his own suite, then spent the rest of the night pacing.

"You didn't answer me," Tim said. "You're a man in love."

"I didn't know it was a question." He settled in behind his desk and started rummaging through the paperwork.

"Ah, but you didn't disagree, either."

Ken leaned back, the leather of his desk chair creaking. "Nothing to argue about." He knew the smile on his face was coming through in his voice.

"Man, what did I tell you?"

"You were right." It felt good to say it out loud. "I love her. I still do. I guess I always have."

"I knew revenge wasn't your game."

"It's not. But I'm not sure love is, either."

"What do you mean?"

"Nothing." He gestured loosely in the air. "I don't mean anything."

That was a lie, of course. He'd switched from wanting to punish her to wanting to love her. The anger that had started out as a lump in his stomach had completely dissolved.

And that meant there was nothing to hold on to. No safety net. He was fully exposed and flying blind. Because the truth of it was, while he might be falling in love, he had absolutely no idea how Lisa felt.

For her, this could be just a game. Sex games, she'd called it that first night. He wouldn't know how she felt until he told her he loved her. And he wouldn't know if she'd stay until he asked her to.

13

"THIS PLACE IS AMAZING." Lisa turned in a circle in the garden of the Greystone Mansion. Once a private residence, the stately building and grounds were now a public park. "Are you sure it's not one of the locations you have in mind for the movie?"

"Nope. This one's just for you and me."

She smiled up at him. "Thank you. I love it here."

"It's one of my favorite places to come when I want to just walk around and think." Taking her hand, he led her through the garden to the koi pond. The giant fish glided through the water, darting among the lily pads and water flowers.

"It must have been fabulous when someone lived in it. I bet the owner was a movie star or director." She tugged at his hand, urging him to a nearby window. "And they threw fabulous parties," she continued, smiling playfully. "And girls in flapper dresses danced the Charleston to a live band playing in the ballroom."

"I bet you're right." He laughed, pulling her around to face him, then planting a kiss right on her mouth. He would have liked to live someplace like that himself. Actually, he would have been happy with someplace smaller. A little yard, maybe a pond in the backyard. But that was an old dream, one he'd abandoned five years ago.

"I'm always right."

He raised his eyebrows. "Are you?"

"Well. I'm always right about the things I'm right about."

Lord, he loved this woman. It felt good to acknowledge, even if only to himself. He pulled her even closer, burying his kisses in her hair. "You're insane. You know that, don't you?"

She leaned back long enough to flash him a winning smile. "I think the word you're looking for is eccentric."

"Oh, is that it?"

She punched him playfully in the arm.

"Well," he said, "you may be eccentric, but I'm hungry."

"And…"

"And it just so happens I have a picnic basket in the trunk of the car."

It was her turn to laugh, then plant a kiss on him. "Did you spend hours planning the perfect afternoon? Or does it just come naturally to you?"

"Which answer would impress you most?"

She didn't answer and neither did he. Instead they headed to the car, retrieved the basket and sheet he'd thrown into the trunk, then returned to the grounds to set up.

"There's a picnic table over there." He pointed across the grounds to a stone table and bench.

Shaking her head, she spread the sheet out on the grass. "This is more traditional."

"Fair enough. As long as we don't have to invite the ants."

As they got comfortable on the sheet, laughing and talking as they dug into the wonderful sandwiches and fruit salad that Tim had prepared, Ken was certain he'd made the right decision coming here. This was nice. Normal. Romantic.

"So, why'd you give up on the diner?"

He looked up, startled. She was lying on her back, eating grapes. Now she turned her head to look at him more directly.

"You were so enthusiastic before...before I left. Why didn't you do it?"

"I don't know. Lack of interest, I guess."

"Oh." She frowned.

"I mean, Oxygen was doing so well. It seemed silly to branch out so differently."

"But you'd always talked about it. Someplace your mom would have loved."

"Yes, well, I lost my enthusiasm."

Little wrinkles appeared on her forehead as she frowned. "Because of me?"

He considered lying to her, but she deserved better than that. "A lot of reasons, but, yes, you were one." He'd realized after Lisa had walked away how much that diner had been for *them* as much as a tribute to his parents. He'd wanted someplace that felt like the home he'd lost when his parents had died. But he'd realized it wouldn't feel like a real home once she had gone, and had abandoned the diner project and moved into the Bellisimo. The old saying was right—you couldn't go home again.

Her hand closed over his. "I'm sorry."

"I know you are. I understand."

Her brow furrowed. "Do you? Do you really?"

"I think so." He shifted, then propped himself up an elbow as he looked at her. "I loved you. You know that, don't you?"

She nodded, her eyes downcast.

"And when you left, it ripped me to shreds." He took a deep breath. "But I don't think you loved me, too. Did you?"

Her eyes met his, and he could see the tears hanging on her lashes. "I don't know. I just..." She shook her head. "I told myself I didn't love you. I couldn't love you."

"Because of your career."

"It means everything to me."

Means or meant? He almost asked, but decided to leave that question for another day. "I know. I always understood your ambition." He grinned. "Under the circumstances, how could I not?"

"I know. That's one of the things about you I loved."

"So there was a little love there."

She blushed. "More than a little. I was just afraid to admit it. And after I left..." She shrugged. "Well, then I was afraid you hated me."

He shook his head. "I tried. But no. I could never hate you. I wanted to." He grinned, trying to lighten the moment. "The most I managed was extremely pissed off."

"Extremely, huh?"

"Maybe more than extremely."

A slight smile touched her lips. "And now?"

He sat up and took her hand. "A lot of things have changed in the past few days." He nodded toward the picnic basket. "And if we're going to make a dent in this food, we'd better start working harder."

She accepted the change of subject, opening up the picnic basket and passing him another sandwich. "I talked to Winston. He's impressed with all the places I've locked in. And I've been faxing him notes on the script, too. He said they were really useful. I think he's pretty pleased with me overall."

"He should be. You've worked hard. What places have you locked in?"

She started counting out on her fingers. "The pier. I talked to the city about getting a permit and that won't be any problem. And Maria's. I called her yesterday, and she's thrilled. And I even locked in your competition—that place with the big band."

"That's great."

"And, of course, I got Oxygen, which impresses Winston most of all."

"I know. I think he's been impressed since day one."

A wave of confusion passed over her face. "What do you mean?"

He told her about Alicia Duncan, and her assumption that Lisa had slept her way into Oxygen.

"But, Ken! She's right!" She stood and started pacing, her hands twisting knots in her I Love L.A. T-shirt. "I can't afford another scandal. Not after Tyrell. Not when I'm just starting to get my career back on track."

He was on his feet and at her side immediately. "Hey, shh. It'll be okay. Alicia's source has to be someone who talks with Winston, so unless you told him, Alicia doesn't know. Not really. That's just the way her mind works. And I told her if she printed anything derogatory about you, not only would she never film inside Oxygen, but I'd see her in court."

She flashed him a watery smile. "You really said that?"

"I meant it, too."

"Thanks."

"It will be okay. Really. Alicia's just grasping at straws, trying to find a way to get to me through you." He turned her around, then urged her chin up with the tip of his finger. "I won't let anything happen to you. Okay?"

She sniffed and blinked, but nodded. "Okay."

He smiled, trying to lighten the moment. "And speaking of sex scandals…"

"What?"

"I want to apologize for last night."

Pure confusion lined her face. "Are you nuts? I had a fabulous time."

"Yeah? Well, so did I."

"Then why the apology?"

He tucked a strand of hair behind her ear. "It was

just so...urgent. You deserve better. Wine and roses. Not lust and...well, lust."

She laughed, all evidence of her earlier worries evaporating. "You're priceless." She stepped closer, then ran her hands through his hair before brushing her lips over his. "Last night was wonderful. And sometimes lust and lust is everything a girl needs."

"I'm glad to hear that," he whispered. "Even so, I'd like to make it up to you."

"You would?" Her voice was breathless, the desire in her eyes electric.

"Oh, yes." He slipped his arm around her waist, stroking the soft flesh under the hem of her shirt and wishing he could touch every smooth inch of her right then.

She smiled. "Who am I to argue, especially if it gets me wine and roses?"

"KEN, THIS IS LOVELY, but you shouldn't." The necklace was amazing—a diamond-studded heart pendant on a simple gold chain. She let it dangle from her fingers, the facets catching the light from the display case and sending rainbows shooting across the room. "It's too much."

"I want to."

She swallowed, feeling spoiled and cherished. "I should say no. I should turn it down."

Gently he took the necklace from her hand, then looped it around her neck and fastened the clasp. Immediately her hand went to her throat, covering the pendant as tears came to her eyes.

"But you won't," he said. "You won't, because you know I want you to have it."

She nodded, unable to speak.

He turned to the salesclerk. "I think that's a yes."

"It's very lovely," the clerk said.

"Not as lovely as the woman wearing it."

She couldn't quite meet his eyes, sure that if she did, she'd burst into tears, as if her body couldn't hold in the whirlwind of emotions and needed release.

As he steered her out to the lobby bar, she managed a smile that she hoped conveyed how happy he'd made her—how happy he'd made her for the past few days now.

"I feel like a princess. I thought I was supposed to get roses, not diamonds."

His smile was pure sin. "Ah, well, the roses are in my room."

"Oh, really?" She cocked an eyebrow as she sank into a wonderfully overstuffed leather armchair.

"Really." He stroked her cheek, and she turned her head toward him, wanting to prolong the contact. Everything she used to feel had flooded back—everything and more. Before, she'd managed to keep up barriers, to stop herself from falling too hard. And that distance had given her the strength to walk away.

Now she was falling hard and fast, like Alice down the rabbit hole. And the truth of it was, she didn't mind. She wanted to fall, wanted to fall right into Ken's arms. And the miracle of it was he seemed to want it, too. After everything she'd done, after all the ways she'd hurt him, he loved her still.

True, he hadn't said so. But he almost had. And nothing in the world would make her believe he was simply playing a revenge game. Maybe he'd started out with that goal—maybe they both had—but somewhere along the way things had changed. Somehow, she'd gotten Ken back.

She'd come back for her career, and she'd found love. She didn't know if she could make the two fit together, but she could enjoy what they had now, and worry about that later.

Ken must have signaled the waitress, because she arrived with two glasses of wine. "You okay?" He passed her a glass. "You look pensive."

"Just tired." That wasn't a lie. She *was* tired. She'd spent the whole night reliving their encounter above Mulholland, getting herself far too worked up to sleep.

"Rough night?" A knowing smile touched his lips.

She met his eyes, her own smile matching his. "I had things other than sleep on my mind."

"I know what you mean." His hand roamed up her thigh. "You should have worn the dress."

A bubble of laughter rose in her throat. "For a picnic?"

His fingers crept higher, heat spreading through her despite the thick denim of her jeans. "I shouldn't have told you where we were going. Maybe you would have worn a skirt." His devilish grin made it to his eyes. "Even on no sleep, I still have other things on my mind."

"Ken..." Her cheeks warmed, and she cast a

glance around to see if they had an audience. "Anyone might see."

"So let them look. They'll just be jealous. Unless…"

Something in his voice piqued her interest. "Unless what?"

"Unless you'd care to go someplace more private?"

"Someplace?"

He stood up, his hand reaching to help her up. "Your place or mine?"

She swallowed, somehow knowing that this was the biggest step of all. They'd had sex on the bench last night. There'd been emotion there, true, but it had been lust and lust, just as Ken had said. Fabulous, but still the direct result of his torment of her over the past few days. He'd teased and tempted, and they'd both finally exploded.

Things had changed between them. She knew that, felt it in her heart. But if she took his hand now—if she went upstairs with him—they wouldn't have sex; they'd make love. And that would be like admitting it out loud.

Lifting her head, she met his eyes. Deep blue, they hid a lot. But he couldn't hide the truth. He wanted this as much as she did. He loved her, and he wouldn't hurt her.

She only hoped that, at the end of the day, she wouldn't hurt him again.

"YOU'RE BEAUTIFUL," he said, delighted with the blush that rose on her cheeks.

"You make me feel beautiful."

"Good." He pulled her to him, then wrapped his arm around her waist. He wanted to make love to her all night, wanted to convince her with his touches that he loved her. And most of all he wanted her to say she loved him, wanted to hear it out loud. "Can I give you the grand tour?"

"I'd like that."

With Lisa's arm linked through his, he walked her through the living area, then into the kitchen.

"Awfully small for the famous Ken Harper, restaurateur extraordinaire."

"Yeah, well, I keep my big kitchen down below."

"Uh-huh." She turned in a slow circle, her eyes taking in the two main rooms. He knew what she saw. The sterile rooms of a man who lived in a hotel. A week ago the rooms had seemed to fit him. Now, however, they just seemed claustrophobic.

"Ken?" She squeezed his hand. "Something wrong?"

"Not a thing." He smiled, shaking off the mood.

"Well, I don't think we're quite done with the tour." She licked her lips. "Are we?"

"No." He stroked his finger across the back of her neck. "We've still got one more room. Would you like to see it?"

She didn't say anything, just stepped out of the kitchen and into the living area. "Are you coming?" She tossed the words back with a grin.

Oh, yes. He was coming. He caught up to her, and they walked through the doorway together. In front of him, the bed loomed. The maid had turned the spread back, and the bit of white sheet seemed to beckon.

He wanted Lisa on that bed, wanted to worship her with his body, wanted her to know how much had changed over the past few days and how much he still loved her.

Wordlessly, he led her to the bed, stroking her arms as she sat on the edge. Hooking a finger under the hem of her shirt, he urged it over her head until she was sitting in front of him in her jeans and a lacy bra. The sight of her nipples, taut against the peach-colored lace, set his blood to burning, and he felt himself harden as the tiny bit of control he'd been clinging to slipped through his fingers.

"Oh, baby." Kneeling in front of her, he fumbled at the button on her jeans, then urged the zipper down. Her fingers splayed through his hair, caressing him, as her breaths came faster and faster.

When he urged her, she lifted her hips, and he pulled her jeans down. She kicked off her shoes and he freed her from the denim, then pressed his face against the cool, soft skin of her inner thigh.

Turning his head, he urged her legs wider as he trailed kisses upward. As he reached the satin of her panties, he slipped his finger underneath, inching them down. Her breath quickened, her moans whispers against his ear as she lifted her hips to help him.

Her sweet musky scent enveloped him, making him giddy and dizzy with lust. He needed to taste her, to kiss her secret places and feel her writhe beneath his touch. He wanted to take her to the absolute height of pleasure, and then follow right after her.

He kissed her intimately, breathing in her erotic scent, as she gasped and squirmed beneath him.

"Ken..." Her voice was low, barely a whisper, but the passion came through loud and clear. "Oh, yes...yes..."

With one hand under her hips, he reached up with his other to stroke her breast. She arched against him, her body tense, and he knew she was close to the edge. He dipped his tongue lower, deeper, tasting and teasing her until, finally, she rocked beneath him, her own pleasure coming close to urging him over the edge himself.

He held her tight, and as she clung to him, he knew that, more than anything—more than his restaurant, more than his career—he wanted this woman in his life.

14

LISA TREMBLED as Ken's arms closed around her. Right on the heels of making love to her with his mouth, he'd made love to her with his body, bringing her again over the edge while he'd held himself in check. She was completely and totally satisfied, and she squirmed against him, reveling in the way he pulled her close. "Your turn," she murmured, wanting to show him with her body how much she felt in her heart.

"Sweetheart, I'd love for it to be my turn, but this is your evening."

She rolled over, quirking a brow. "Doesn't seem quite fair," she said, sliding her hand lower to see if he was still aroused. She found the hard length of him under the sheet and ran her fingers down, teasing him.

He sucked in a breath, the effort of concentration apparent on his face. "This was my gift to you, remember? To make up for...well..." His breath was ragged against her ear. "You know."

"Oh, I know." She slipped her hand under the sheet, feeling his velvety smoothness against her palm. "The thing is, I was thinking about changing that little deal."

She tightened her fingers around him, watching his face, watching the way he closed his eyes as control slipped away. A wave of power broke over her. He wanted her, and he was going crazy simply from her touch. She wanted to take him to the edge, needed to know she'd taken him there.

Slowly, she crawled on top of him, lowering her lips to his as their bodies, still slick from their earlier lovemaking, glided together.

She didn't want to wait, couldn't wait, and she lowered herself onto him, crying out when he thrust upward. As she rocked above him, never letting up the pace, giving him no chance to hold back, he drove deeper and deeper until both of them had reached the point of no return. Moving frantically to the same rhythm, they found release at the same exquisite moment. When the ripples of pleasure finally subsided, they collapsed against each other, warm and sated.

She rolled off him, and he spooned against her.

"I love you," he said, the whisper of his voice soft against her neck.

She smiled against the pillow and tightened her grip on his arms that held her close. But even though she opened her mouth to say it back, the words wouldn't come. She was too scared of being wrong. Too scared of sacrificing everything she'd worked for.

And when she rolled over to face him, still silent, she saw the disappointment in his eyes. But she also saw hope. And seeing that, she knew she'd love him forever.

She gave him a tender kiss on the cheek, then

rolled back over, pressing her body against his. His arm closed around her, pulling her close, and she said a silent prayer that someday, sometime, she'd have the courage to tell him she loved him. The courage to say it out loud.

THEY'D FORGOTTEN to close the curtains, and now the morning sun streamed through the window sheers, glinting off her hair, fanned over her pillow. Lost in sleep, she looked beautiful, her lips still moist and swollen from his kisses. Ken's fingers itched to touch her. To wake her up and sink into her once again. To make love to her over and over until she finally said the words back. Until she finally told him what he was already certain of—that she loved him.

But that wasn't something he could force or rush. He knew she loved him—knew it in his heart—but until she realized it herself, it would never be real. And for her to discover it, he needed to give her space and time to think.

He didn't want to leave her, but he'd been neglecting the restaurant long enough. Fighting every resisting muscle, he dragged himself out of bed. Not only was leaving her warmth torture, but after only three hours of sleep, leaving his bed—any bed—was pure torment.

Next to him, Lisa stirred, and the movement was almost enough to make him change his mind. He held his breath, knowing that if she so much as opened an eye or smiled in her sleep, he'd lose all self-control and crawl back under the covers, pull her close, and lose himself in her sweetness.

No. He was a responsible business owner. About time he went and had a look at how his livelihood was faring in his absence.

Not that he was really concerned. His people were the best, and Tim could run Oxygen with his eyes closed. Still, Ken had never been comfortable delegating authority, and he'd left the day-to-day operations in someone else's hands long enough.

Quietly, so as not to wake her, he sat up, then padded naked to the closet. He rummaged in the semi-darkness, needing to find something to wear but not wanting to disturb her.

Finally dressed, he headed to the door, pausing just long enough to look back at her.

"I love you, Lisa Neal," he whispered. "So help me, I do."

SO HELP HIM.

As soon as she heard the door click shut, Lisa rolled over, hugging her pillow to her chest. When she reached up to push her hair out of her face, her hand came away wet, and she realized she was crying.

She was making this so difficult. Lots of people juggled careers and family. But she wasn't most people. She knew herself. She wouldn't feel right—wouldn't feel whole—until she was certain her career was on the right track. And that wasn't something Ken could help with. And it certainly wouldn't be fair to him to tell him she loved him. What was love, after all, if she couldn't back it up with action? If she wasn't willing to give it her everything?

And she couldn't. Not now. She needed to make something of herself. If she backed away from her dreams for him—even just a little—she'd just end up resenting him. She'd seen it happen in her own family, and she didn't want it to happen to her. Not to Lisa Neal, the girl who always accomplished whatever she set her mind to. For five years she'd been struggling, and now she had a real chance. She intended to hold on tight and not let go.

It just wasn't fair. Five years ago she was still young and naive enough to actually convince herself that she *didn't* love him. A lie, of course, but one she'd bought into. But she was older now. Smarter. Now she *knew* she loved him. Now she knew how terrifying love could be.

Sitting up, she wrapped the sheet around her, remembering the way his hands had felt on her. *Ken's hands.* Maybe she was selling him short. Of all the men in the world, Ken understood ambition. Maybe it could work. Maybe, together, they could make it work.

Or maybe she was just grasping at straws in the aftermath of passion.

The phone rang, and she reached for it, assuming it would be Ken. It wasn't.

"Ms. Neal?"

"Yes?" She frowned, wondering who on earth would have found her in Ken's room.

"This is the front desk. Mr. Harper left instructions

to inform you if any messages were in your hotel voice mail. Shall I patch you in?''

''Yes, please.'' An electronic beeping ensued, followed by a generic message, and then Winston's voice was asking her to call as soon as she was free.

Gnawing on her lip and wondering what current crisis he was facing, she hung up and immediately dialed New York.

''Lisa!'' Winston's voice was just as exuberant over the phone as it was in person.

''What's up?''

''I've got a little proposition for you, my dear. I think you're going to like it.''

A chill raced up her spine, and a lump settled in her stomach. ''Okay...''

''How'd you like to work for me, be a development exec here at Avenue F? You'd be my right hand. Office overlooking Central Park. Power to green-light my films. The whole nine yards.''

She held the receiver out and stared at the phone, trying to process what he'd just said.

''Lisa?'' His voice, far away and tinny, seemed alarmed.

She yanked the phone back and pressed it to her ear, still unbelieving. ''You want to hire me? At your production company? To work in Manhattan? With you?''

''I always knew you were a smart kid.''

''But...'' She snapped her mouth shut, trying to decide if the room had always been spinning or if that was a new development. ''Are you saying...'' She took a deep breath and tried again. "You mean, you want to hire me permanently? Not just on the crew of *Velvet Bed II*? Read scripts? Develop projects? Go to work everyday to your offices across from Central Park?"

"That's it, kid. You know my assistant, Daniel?" He didn't wait for an answer. "Well, he got an offer from the BBC. He's moving to London and leaving me in a lurch. I thought of you, kid."

"Me?"

"We'd be working close together. Daily meetings. That kind of thing. You'd be right in the thick of things. You interested?"

She pinched herself. Wondering if she was dreaming. Winston was offering her exactly what she'd wanted—a development position. Power. Control. And at a stellar company with two Oscars under its belt. Avenue F had deals with all the major studios. She couldn't have crafted a better job if she tried.

"Why me?" She frowned, wondering if she was an idiot to question fate, but needing to know. "I mean, I had to beg you to give me a shot on just one movie."

"You told me you were good. And now you've proved it. You've done a heck of a job lining up locations in Los Angeles. I like the notes you've sent back on the script. You've got good ideas about casting. I like what I see."

"And?"

He chuckled. "And I checked you out a little bit more. You're right. You're one of the ones Tyrell screwed. So what do you say? You wanna make movie history?''

She certainly did. And she opened her mouth to say yes. But something held her back. "I need... Can I call you tomorrow?"

She held her breath, afraid he'd tell her to take it or leave it, now or never. Instead he just said, "Sure."

She hung up, exhaling in relief and not at all sure what she'd just done or why'd she'd done it. All she knew for certain was that she needed to see Ken.

15

WHEN HE UNLOCKED THE DOOR to his office and stepped inside, Ken was in a perfectly good mood. Two seconds later Alicia walked through the doorway, and his entire day went to hell.

"Not now, Alicia. I'm really not in the mood to argue with you."

"Good." She threw her purse on his desk and sat in a chair, facing him dead-on. "Because I really don't think you should be arguing."

He rubbed his hands over his face, wishing he'd stayed in bed with Lisa. "What do you want now, Alicia?"

"Same thing I wanted before. And when I'm done, you're going to wish you'd agreed from day one."

"What are you talking about?"

"Ken, sweetie, a picture is worth a thousand words." She rummaged in her tote bag, finally emerging with a manila folder. She slid it across the desk to him.

Black-and-white glossy photos. He and Lisa. On Mulholland. And it was very, very obvious what they were doing.

"So?" He hoped he sounded calm, despite the pounding of his heart in his chest.

"So, I wonder how pleased Miss Neal or Mr. Miller will be to see these pictures published in *Variety* or the *Hollywood Reporter*? I can see the headline now—'Avenue F Location Scout Uses Unique Methods To Close Deals.'"

"You wouldn't."

Her smile was icy. "Come on, Ken. You know me better than that. I most certainly would."

He ran his hands through his hair, then thumbed through the photos. Lisa couldn't afford another scandal, especially not one that centered around her. She'd already lost years of her career because of the Tyrell debacle. Ken didn't intend to let her career die because of another scandal, not one that he caused.

Dammit, he loved Lisa, even more than before, if that were possible. And he'd do anything in his power to see that she didn't get hurt.

He took a deep breath, knowing exactly what he was giving up. "Okay. You win."

"I always win," she purred, her supercilious smile making him almost reconsider.

"When we open the restaurant up to film the movie, why don't you shoot an episode of your show here? That way you not only get to air the first shot of the inside of Oxygen, but you can interview some of the cast and crew of *The Velvet Bed*, too."

She cocked her head, as if looking for the hitch. "That's it? No strings? You're just going to let me film here? Open access, plus the movie? Film whatever I want and talk to whomever I want?''

''One string.''

''I knew it.''

''You return the photos and the negatives. You sign an agreement to never disclose what you saw.''

''These photos are one heck of a story.''

''No, they're not. They're trash journalism. And I'm betting you don't want to go there.''

Her mouth thinned as she inspected her fingernails. ''Tell me this, then. Why?''

He scowled. ''Why what?''

''For five years, you've kept this place more secure than the Pentagon. Now suddenly you're opening it up to a film crew, and to me. It goes entirely against everything you've done over your whole career.''

''I think my career will survive. It'll lose a little mystique, sure. But I'll gain some publicity.'' He shrugged, deciding maybe he even believed that. ''Doesn't matter, anyway. My career's not my primary concern right now.''

Her mouth thinned. ''She's not worth it. She's a little tramp, not even worth worrying about. And your career will be safe. She's the one who'll be smeared. She's using you, Ken. Don't you see that? I only want to protect you.''

''She's not using me, Alicia. I love her. I always have.''

Alicia flinched, and he understood. Jealousy. ''There's nothing between us, Alicia. You and me. There never was.''

"Of course there was, Kenny." She smiled, her teeth dazzling for the camera. "We were perfect together."

"No. I'm sorry. We had some nice times, but there's nothing there."

She ran her tongue over her lips, her eyes not meeting his. "You don't love me—don't even care for me—and yet you love this Lisa person?"

"I love her."

She tossed her head back, her thick coat of makeup catching the light. "She's not worth it, you know."

"Well, that's where you and I disagree." He held out his hand. "The pictures?"

He could practically see the wheels turning—weighing a fit of jealous revenge against a stellar career opportunity. "All right," she said finally. "It's a deal. No story, no photos."

"Thank you. And for the record, if a stray photo or comment gets out, I'll sue you for every last dime you have."

"Why, Kenny, and here I thought we were friends."

"I mean it." He smiled, trying to take the edge off his words. He wasn't sure he completely trusted Alicia, but he did know that she wouldn't do anything to risk her own reputation, which meant, at least for now, Lisa was safe.

"She doesn't love you, you know. Lisa Neal loves herself." Her sardonic smile caught him by surprise. "Trust me, sweetie. I know the type."

"She's not like you." But he wasn't so sure. She'd

left him for her career once before. Did he really think she'd changed so much? They'd had a few nice moments, sure, but did he really think that gave him the world?

He shook his head, frustrated. He wanted to believe in Lisa and, dammit, he would. "Anyway, it doesn't matter. I love her. It's not a give-and-take situation. I'm doing this for her. And because you got in the middle, it looks like you're reaping some of the benefit."

"That's my job, Kenny. To be right in the middle of it."

"The photos?"

She nodded toward the manila envelope. "Keep them."

"I mean it. Not one word."

"You're not even going to tell your little Lisa?"

"What? That a reporter photographed her half-naked on a bench above Mulholland Drive? I don't think she needs to know that."

Alicia pushed her chair back and stood. She gave him a long, hard look, then shook her head, bemused.

"What?"

"I just can't figure you out."

He half smiled. "I didn't realize you were trying to."

"Five years ago, everyone said you were a small-town Texas innocent who managed to pick up some business savvy. Now I'm thinking maybe you're just an old-fashioned nice guy."

"Not something we need to be debating."

"No, it's not." She swung her purse over her shoulder. "Because the fact is, in a town like this, if you're just a nice guy, you're screwed."

EROTIC PICTURES above Mulholland?

Lisa's stomach churned, wondering if it could really be true. She was standing just outside Ken's door, and now slipped further away as Alicia strolled past, jauntily swinging her purse from one finger.

Pictures. Of her and Ken. Oh, Lord, it couldn't be true. And yet it was. She'd heard the discussion, saw the photos pass between them. A wave of coldness swept over her, and she hugged herself, terrified she'd come so close to another scandal.

Raw fury pumped through her veins. Ken's little bargain had put her in a terrible position—trading sex for services. What had he been thinking?

No. Not Ken. *She'd* put herself in the position. She could have said no. But she'd wanted it, wanted Ken. She'd been a fool, a damn fool. And someone who'd already been through one scandal should know enough to not get burned twice.

Leaning over, she propped her hands on her knees and took deep, calming breaths. Another scandal. Oh, Lord, how could she survive another scandal?

Except there wasn't going to be a scandal. Her heart slowed to its normal pace as reality set in. No scandal. She was safe. Ken had rescued her. He'd saved her reputation. She wasn't certain exactly what had happened, but she knew one thing for sure—he'd made a decision this morning, and he'd put her above his career. The knowledge humbled her, and scared her.

She needed to make the same kind of decision, and soon. But she didn't know if she had his strength or his confidence. He'd said his career would still be fine. She wished she could believe the same thing about hers. If she let herself love Ken—

She stopped the thought. The truth was, she already *did* love Ken. So, the question was, if she *admitted* she loved him, if they started a relationship, could she keep her career on track?

He'd taken a risk for her letting Alicia film inside his restaurant. She nibbled her lower lip, wanting to take a risk for him—for love—but her fear held her back. And in the end, she simply stood there as silent tears rolled down her cheeks.

THE REAL ESTATE AGENT stopped in front of the blue bungalow with the white-painted trim and turned to Ken. "Here we are."

He stepped out of the car, then stood on the grass, staring at the cottage. For almost five years he'd lived in the hotel, with no urge to move back into a house, to have a normal life.

But suddenly he couldn't keep thoughts of a home—a real home—out of his head. These past few days with Lisa had made him realize how much he'd given up when she'd left. A home. A family. Even his simple dream of opening a diner.

The agent paused at the door to look back at him, a quizzical expression on her face. "Mr. Harper?"

"Sorry. I'm coming."

The inside of the house was as charming as the outside, and it took only a half hour of looking around to know that he wanted to buy the place.

"Can you have an offer drawn up by tonight?"

The agent's eyes went wide, but she nodded. "Of course."

"Good." He felt better. He was making decisions, getting things done.

He wanted to live in the house with Lisa, and he hoped like hell she'd agree. But even if she didn't, it was time he started living his life like a life again.

It was a lesson he'd learned the hard way. He only hoped that, over the past five years, Lisa had learned the same thing.

BY THE TIME Ken got back to his suite, Lisa had pretty much paced a hole in the carpet.

"Where'd you go?"

"No place special." A curious smile touched his lips. "I just bought a little house in Santa Monica."

"You bought a house?" She couldn't help the delighted laugh that escaped. "Just like that, you bought a house?"

"Yup. A little blue cottage on one of those streets you think are so cute." He shrugged. "Actually, I just made an offer. But I think the owners will accept it."

"I...why?"

"A lot of reasons. Mostly, I want a life." In two long strides he was by her side and holding her hands. "I want one with you."

She swallowed, her chest tightening. "With me?"

"I love you, Lisa. I want you to stay with me."

Her heart swelled. He'd said it before, but that was in the heat of passion. Now to hear him say it, to say he wanted a life with her...

A wave of happiness washed over, only to be followed by the crush of reality. The past was repeating itself, and in her purse she had a plane ticket for New York.

"I...but..." Taking a deep breath, she steeled herself. "You should have talked to me first. You can't just buy us a house—"

"Me. I bought me a house."

"But you said..."

"I said I love you. I said I want a life with you. But if you say no, I'm still moving. I've been in limbo for five years. It's time I started living again—living my life, not just my job. And, Lisa, the truth is, I can do both."

She pressed her lips together, fighting another round of tears. She'd been mulling it over for hours, and the decision she'd finally made wasn't any easier now than it had been an hour ago. "Can you? Can you get where you want to be and still have a relationship? Can you do that and not resent me for taking time away from your ambitions?"

"I'm already where I want to be."

She nodded. "And that's the problem. Don't you see? I never made it like you did. I never tasted success and I want the chance. It's what I've always wanted, and I'm not prepared to give it up."

"Do you have to give it up if we're together?"

"I...I do love you. So much I..." A tear rolled down her cheek and she wiped it away. "But I don't want to end up resenting you. I couldn't live with that." She took a deep breath, wishing she could make him understand how difficult it was for her. How much she needed to focus in order to succeed. "I—I'm thinking about heading back to New York."

For just a moment his brow furrowed before his face cleared. "I thought you were looking to move back here."

"I was." She had been. But Winston's opportunity was too good to pass up. She shrugged. "I figured I needed to be here to get my career back on track. I was wrong."

"What happened?"

"Winston. He offered me a job as a development executive. Avenue F is a major company. It's exactly what I've wanted."

"So that's it? You're just going to go back to New York? Forget about everything that's happened between us?"

Her eyes burned, but she refused to cry. "I'll never forget these past few days. But I also never lied to you. You've known from the day I got here what my priority is."

"Sweetheart, I've known from before then. And I see your priorities haven't changed."

"And yours have?" The minute she said the words, she regretted it. His priorities *had* changed. Just that morning he'd saved her reputation and agreed to open his restaurant to that horrible Alicia woman.

"Yeah, they have." He took her hand, urging her to sit next to him on the couch. "Sweetheart, why? Why not stay here? Just a couple of days ago, you were telling me how much you miss Los Angeles."

"I miss having a career even more. Can't you understand? This is everything I've dreamed of, everything I've wanted. The chance to make movies, to be a player. For five years I've felt useless, like I didn't even have a purpose for being on the planet. And now I do."

"Maybe your purpose is to be with me."

She blinked back a tear, but didn't answer.

Ken shook the comment off. "Sorry, that's not fair. Of course you have to do what you love. But this isn't your only shot. Winston knows you'll have offers coming out of your ears. He's just trying to lock you in. There will be other offers."

"Can you promise me that? Can you put it in writing and swear to me I'll find work if I tell Winston no?"

He took a deep breath, then shook his head. "No. All I can tell you is I love you."

"I know." She swallowed, wanting to throw her arms around his neck and cry until she couldn't cry any more. Instead she sat up straighter, knowing she was going to hurt him, but unable to help that. "I know. I—I love you, too." Tears streamed down her face, but she didn't wipe them away. "The thing is, I just don't think that love is enough."

16

LISA PRESSED her forehead against the glass, looking down twenty floors from her office to watch a horse-drawn carriage head into Central Park. The intercom buzzed. "Ms. Neal? It's Mr. Scorcese's agent."

"Thanks."

She turned around and picked up the phone, then spent the next ten minutes hashing out the basics of a directing deal for a new film Avenue F was developing. When she finally hung up, she fell exhausted into the chair behind her desk. In front of her, scripts and contracts were piled up, leaving not even a square inch of desktop.

Three weeks back in New York. The *Velvet Bed* sequel was heavy into preproduction. She was juggling six other projects. That morning alone she'd talked to executives at Universal, Paramount and Warner Brothers.

In other words, she was doing exactly what she'd always wanted. Finally, she was living her dream.

She should be ecstatic. Instead she just felt hollow.

The intercom buzzed again. "Ms. Neal? It's Greg."

She snatched up the phone, happier than she'd been in weeks. "Hey! Where are you?"

"Still in L.A. How's the Big Apple?"

"Fabulous. It's great. I love it."

"Uh-huh."

"What's that supposed to mean?"

"Nothing," Greg said quickly. "I'm just distracted." Silence filled the line, and then, "Have you talked to him?"

Tears welled, and she ran the side of her finger under her eyes. "No. I—I haven't reached him." Actually, she hadn't tried. She'd been too afraid of what he'd say if she called.

"I went to the anniversary celebration at Oxygen," he said.

"You did?" Her throat felt parched, and she reached for the diet Coke can on her desk. "How was it?"

"Fine. Ken looked good."

"Oh." She pressed her lips together, trying to not cry. "Is he still living in the Bellisimo?"

"Not according to the paper," Greg said. "Last month's issue said he bought a house in Santa Monica. Oxygen's doing better than ever. He's even opening one in the Valley. Studio City, I think."

"Oh." He was doing exactly what he said he would. Getting on with his life. Balancing a life with his career. She wondered if he mowed his own lawn. Even more than that, she wondered if he was dating. Somehow, she couldn't bring herself to ask Greg that.

"So, what's your mom say?" Greg asked.

"She thinks it's great." When Lisa had called to tell her mom and sister that she'd taken a position as a development executive, they'd been happy for her. But somehow, the thrill she'd always expected to hear wasn't there. Her mom was proud, sure. But nothing felt different.

"But...?"

"Nothing. I just realized that I'm the only one who cares. I mean, they're glad I have a job, but so long as I like it, they're happy."

"Well, it is your life."

"I know. And I always thought I knew exactly what I wanted. And now that I have it..." She shrugged, even though Greg couldn't see her.

"You're not sure you want it?"

"No. I want it." Now that she'd tasted it, she wanted it more than ever, if that were possible. "This is my life. It's what I do, who I am, and I love it. I really do. I just...I just wonder if I don't love Ken even more."

And she wondered if she'd made the biggest mistake of her life walking away. Most of all, though, she wondered if she could fix it.

"I'M GLAD YOU REVISED the plans," Tim said. "This location's much better suited for a diner than a restaurant like Oxygen."

Ken shifted his hard hat as he looked at the plans spread out on the dusty table. The day after Lisa left, he'd closed the lease for this site then completely revamped the concept for the restaurant, deciding the Studio City location was going to be a diner.

"You need to find me someone to help with the menu."

"Someone!" Tim looked shocked. "That's a task I'll happily take over."

"Uh-huh." Ken grimaced. "Nothing personal, but we want burgers and fries here. Not veal and caviar."

"Trust me. An *artiste* is always right."

Ken smiled, but his heart wasn't in it. A familiar wave of melancholy washed over him, and he focused on the plans, trying to get his head back together.

"She's doing what she has to do."

He nodded. "I know. I'd just hoped..." He shrugged. "I guess I'd hoped that after she left she'd come back. That she'd walk through the door of the anniversary party and we'd start over."

"And you were hoping she'd be the one looking at these plans with you instead of me."

"Nothing personal."

"No offense," Tim said. "I don't look nearly as good in a dress as she does. Though I think this hard hat does give me some allure." He struck a Mr. Universe pose. "What do you think? The women are going to start coming in droves, right?"

Ken didn't laugh, but he did crack a smile, and for that he was grateful. He checked his watch. "It's almost four. I need to get home and see if the workmen need anything." He was having the kitchen renovated, and the contractor always seemed to have questions at the end of the day.

"You're just rebuilding everything these days."

"Metaphor for my life." Maybe if he built something new, he'd finally forget about the old. Though he doubted it. Even more so than when she'd left the first time, Lisa was ingrained in his heart and etched in his soul.

It was his own fault, of course. Only an idiot would concoct a revenge-by-sex scheme and assume that he could walk away unscathed. He was an idiot, all right. An idiot completely in love with a woman who didn't love him. No, she loved him. She just didn't realize how much.

"You could fly to New York, you know. Convince her. Even try the bicoastal thing."

Ken nodded. "I thought about it. But it's not just the distance—it's everything she believes, it's everything she wants. I mean, she told me she loved me. But she also told me it doesn't matter, because she needs to focus on her career." He looked Tim in the eye. "She doesn't want me in New York. She doesn't even want to try."

"So what are you going to do?"

Ken shrugged, his shoulders heavy from the weight of his melancholy. "Miss her. Love her. Get on with my life." Even though the last thing he wanted was a life without Lisa. "And keep believing that it's not over. I saw her eyes. I know she loves me. And even though I don't think she's realized it, I know she's changed." He looked Tim in the eye. "She will come back."

"I hope you're right."

Ken nodded. So did he. More than anything, so did he.

Finished at the diner, he headed back toward Santa Monica. Traffic on the 405 was murder, of course, and that just added to his already foul mood.

Once inside, he headed straight for the kitchen to face the day's minicrisis. Today's was wallpaper.

"This, or this?" Arnold asked, holding up two sample sheets.

Ken wasn't in the mood to choose, his mind on Lisa, not on his walls. "What do you like?"

Arnold shrugged. "I like the thinner stripes but, Tony, he likes the thick better."

"Maybe you should flip a coin."

"You don't have a preference?" Arnold's voice sounded so hopeful.

"Sorry. Not in the mood today." He turned around to leave, hoping to catch a quick nap.

"Maybe we should ask the young lady's opinion."

Ken froze, then turned around to face the older man. "Excuse me?"

"The young lady. On the couch. She's been here for hours."

Ken practically tripped over his feet getting to the living room. And sure enough, there she was.

Lisa. Sitting right there, her hands twisting in her lap. A look of restrained hopefulness on her face.

"Hi, Ken," she said. He saw her take a deep breath. "I came back to say I'm sorry."

"I see." He wanted to keep a poker face, but he was sure surprise and curiosity were leaking through.

"Sorry about what? Sorry about the way you left? Sorry you hurt me? Sorry there can't be anything between us?"

"All of the above," she said and his heart fell. "Except the last."

The wave of disappointment vanished as her words sunk in. "*Except* the last," he repeated, needing to make sure he got it right.

"Right. I mean…if I'm not too late."

"So you're here because…" He couldn't finish the thought, too afraid he was reading her wrong.

She stood. "I've got everything I ever wanted working with Winston. It's been an amazing three weeks. I've had lunch with Oscar-winning directors and actors. I've made deals I only dreamed about. It's been fabulous."

"Congratulations." He knew his voice was tight, but he couldn't help it. "I know that's what you've always wanted. I'm happy for you. Really."

"Yes, well, have you ever heard the saying, 'Be careful what you wish for'?"

He took a deep breath. He needed to know why she was there, and he needed to know now. "What are you telling me, Lisa?"

"I got everything I ever wanted…and then I realized I didn't have everything after all."

"What don't you have?" *Him?* He thought so, but he couldn't ask her outright, didn't want to run the risk of being hurt again.

A smile teased the corner of her mouth. "I need a favor," she said.

"A favor?"

This time it was her turn to take a deep breath. "I need someone to show me around Los Angeles. Permanently, this time."

His heart twisted, and he took a step toward her, wondering if it could really be true. After all this time, had Lisa finally really realized she loved him—and finally understood what that meant? "What are you saying, Lisa? Tell me. In plain English, tell me what you want."

"I want you. Permanently. Here."

"What about your job?"

"I, uh, I quit."

"You quit?"

"I had to." She moved toward him until they were just an arm's length apart. "I had to prove to myself I'm not afraid anymore."

"And now you're not?"

"No. I still am. A little, anyway." She took a deep breath. "I'm going to need a lot of help through this."

The band around his heart loosened. She'd come back to him. He'd had faith in her this time, and he'd been right. "So you're telling me that you can love me. What about resenting me?"

She swallowed, then straightened her shoulders. "I'm making my own choices. There's nothing to resent you for. I just need you here to hold my hand."

He gave her fingers a gentle squeeze. "That's something I'm happy to do." He paused. "So you really quit.'' His Lisa, taking the plunge like that. ''I guess it must be love.''

She looked him in the eye, and he saw the truth reflected in her tears. ''It is.''

''Where are you going to work?''

''At first I didn't know. But after my plane landed, Winston called. He said if I was really serious about moving back to L.A., that he could set me up in an office out here.''

''So you said yes, of course.''

She shook her head. ''No. I told him I'd call him tomorrow. I'll probably take it. But I figured I should think about it. See what my other options are.''

He reached out for her, and she moved easily into his arms. ''I love you, Lisa.''

''I know. I love you, too.'' She pressed her face against his chest.

''About that favor you wanted...'' He couldn't hide the tease in his voice, and she looked up, her eyes wide and playfully wary.

''Yes?''

''I was thinking another quid pro quo.''

Her forehead furrowed. ''Okay...what?''

He let go of her hand long enough to step into his bedroom and take the small velvet box from the top drawer of his bureau. When he came back out, he handed it to her. ''You. You want someone to show you around Los Angeles permanently. I want you.''

She opened the box, her eyes going wide as she saw the solitaire inside. ''Oh, Ken...''

"I wanted to give this to you five years ago. I hope you'll accept it now."

A single tear streamed down her face, but the delight in her eyes erased any fears he had that the tear was other than one of happiness. "Is this a proposal?"

"As a matter of fact, it is."

She slipped her finger through the ring, joy shining in her face. "In that case, this is an acceptance."

Epilogue

Three years later

"YOU'LL BE OKAY?" Lisa nibbled on her lower lip as Tim held out his arms for Claire.

"He's great with kids," Ken said, passing their year-old daughter to the chef. They were in the dining room of Oxygen, where Tim slid into a chair, with Claire happily settled on his lap.

"I know." She flashed Tim a rueful smile. "It's just..."

"It's just you don't trust me."

She laughed. "I do. It's only..."

"My wife's neurotic," Ken said.

"This, I know." Tim bounced Claire. "Is your mommy neurotic? Can you say neurotic?"

"Na ga," Claire gurgled.

Ken squeezed her hand, and Lisa squeezed back. "Come on. We can do this. It's a big night."

She nodded. It was a huge night. The second movie she'd produced for Avenue F—after it landed the deal with Universal Studios—was up for best picture.

"And your limo's not going to wait forever." He stood, clutching Claire to his side. "Now go on. Your daughter and I want to see you up on that stage making one hell of an acceptance speech." He turned to Ken. "And as soon as your mother-in-law gets in, I'll pass Claire and concentrate on the post-ceremony party. There's going to be a hell of a crowd here in a few hours."

"Sorry the plane was delayed."

"Not your problem. And it gives me the chance to bond with my goddaughter." He nodded toward the door. "Now go."

They did, and Lisa couldn't keep her eyes off Ken as they took the stairs from the mezzanine to the lobby. He looked handsome in the tux, but he also looked proud, and she knew that look was for her.

"What?" he asked.

"What?"

"You're staring."

A smile touched her lips. "I just wanted to say thank-you."

"For what?"

"For loving me. For being here."

For three years they'd juggled careers—and a family—as she'd struggled to get Avenue F even more firmly on the map. As it turned out, being in Los Angeles helped, and Winston never let her forget that he'd been generous enough to suggest it.

Even now she was amazed that she could spread herself so thin. But she never felt thin. Not with Ken. Not with Claire. Not with work. They energized her. And she loved them all—her family most of all.

She squeezed his hand. "Thank you for putting up with me."

His laugh delighted her as always, and he pulled her close. "Sweetheart, I'll put up with you forever. I love you, you know."

She nodded. She did know. And, fortunately for her, she'd figured out what that meant before it was too late.

He helped her into the limo, then settled in next to her. "So, are you nervous?"

"Nervous?" she asked, even though she knew exactly what he meant.

"Tonight. It's a big deal."

She half shrugged. "It's just an award, not that big a deal. Between you and Claire, I've already got everything I need."

His arm closed around her shoulders and she leaned in close. "It's a sweet sentiment, but you know I don't believe you."

She couldn't help the laugh that escaped. He knew her so well. "I know." She twisted in his arms to see his eyes. "And you know that's one of the reasons I love you?"

He didn't answer her, just kissed her, but she was more than happy to take that as a yes.

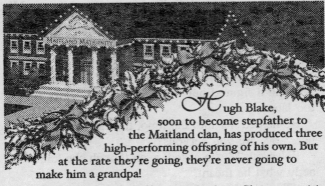

*H*ugh Blake, soon to become stepfather to the Maitland clan, has produced three high-performing offspring of his own. But at the rate they're going, they're never going to make him a grandpa!

There's *Suzanne*, a work-obsessed CEO whose Christmas spirit could use a little topping up....

And *Thomas*, a lawyer whose ability to hold on to the woman he loves is evaporating by the minute....

And *Diane*, a teacher so dedicated to her teenage students she hasn't noticed she's put her own life on hold.

But there's a Christmas wake-up call in store for the Blake siblings. Love *and* Christmas miracles are in store for all three!

Maitland Maternity Christmas

A collection from three of Harlequin's favorite authors

Muriel Jensen
Judy Christenberry
& Tina Leonard

Look for it in November 2001.

Celebrate the season with

A holiday anthology featuring
a classic Christmas story from
New York Times bestselling author

Debbie Macomber

Plus a brand-new *Morgan's Mercenaries* story
from *USA Today* bestselling author

Lindsay McKenna

And a brand-new *Twins on the Doorstep* story
from national bestselling author

Stella Bagwell

Available at your favorite retail outlets in November 2001!

Silhouette®
Where love comes alive™

Visit Silhouette at www.eHarlequin.com   PSMC

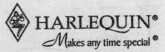

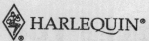

CALL THE ONES YOU LOVE OVER THE HOLIDAYS!

Save $25 off future book purchases when you buy any four Harlequin® or Silhouette® books in October, November and December 2001,

PLUS

receive a phone card good for 15 minutes of long-distance calls to anyone you want in North America!

WHAT AN INCREDIBLE DEAL!

Just fill out this form and attach 4 proofs of purchase (cash register receipts) from October, November and December 2001 books, and Harlequin Books will send you a coupon booklet worth a total savings of $25 off future purchases of Harlequin® and Silhouette® books, AND a 15-minute phone card to call the ones you love, anywhere in North America.

Please send this form, along with your cash register receipts as proofs of purchase, to:
In the USA: Harlequin Books, P.O. Box 9057, Buffalo, NY 14269-9057
In Canada: Harlequin Books, P.O. Box 622, Fort Erie, Ontario L2A 5X3
Cash register receipts must be dated no later than December 31, 2001.
Limit of 1 coupon booklet and phone card per household.
Please allow 4-6 weeks for delivery.

I accept your offer! Please send me my coupon booklet and a 15-minute phone card:

Name: _____

Address: _____ City: _____

State/Prov.: _____ Zip/Postal Code: _____

Account Number (if available): _____

---

097 KJB DAGL
PHQ4012

WITH HARLEQUIN AND SILHOUETTE

There's a romance to fit your every mood.

Passion

Harlequin Temptation

Harlequin Presents

Silhouette Desire

Pure Romance

Harlequin Romance

Silhouette Romance

Home & Family

Harlequin
American Romance

Silhouette
Special Edition

A Longer Story With More

Harlequin
Superromance

Suspense & Adventure

Harlequin Intrigue

Silhouette Intimate
Moments

Humor

Harlequin Duets

Historical

Harlequin Historicals

Special Releases

Other great
romances
to explore